Not What it Seems

Also by Lorne Oliver

Sgt. Reid Series
Red Island
Red Serge

Alcrest Mysteries
The Cistern
The Menu
The Pass
The Chimes

The Alcrest Stories
Wash Forbidden Fruit
Sins of a Vegan

NOT WHAT IT SEEMS

A Faryn Steel Thriller

LORNE OLIVER

NOT WHAT IT SEEMS

ISBN 978-1-7771782-1-5

COVER: FARYN STEEL Photography
Cover Design: Alcrest Services

For Avery.

Welcome to the story.

DAY ONE
SUNDAY

Chapter 1

WILE E. COYOTE CHASED the Roadrunner around my steaming coffee mug. My bare feet were up on the large flower pot on the edge of my deck and I wiggled and stretched my toes. The red polish needed a change. Three stars had been rebelliously tattooed near my left little toe when I was seventeen. Shit, that was so long ago. In the pot was a tree, I don't remember what kind, that I trimmed occasionally and tried the best I could to take care of it. That explained the two bare branches and how it was bent over like a hunchback and dwarfed like a malnourished child. I breathed in the crisp air. The deck was all open with a few pillars and a roof, but no walls or windows. Garth sang about his friends in low places from my phone on the arm of the soft chair I had liberated from a yard sale for five bucks. Calm. There were not going to be many more mornings I could do this before winter came.

Coffee. There had barely been enough milk in the carton, the stability of which was questionable anyway, to change the murky sludge, so I added extra sugar. It made me long for what passed as coffee at police headquarters. I thought about adding something special, but I was on call. This was how a mature woman spent her Sunday morning.

How did a mature woman spend her Saturday night? This one spent it soaking in a scalding hot bubble bath eating chicken wings and smoking a jay. I'm a free willed woman. Single. No kids. Secure in myself enough to know that nothing could beat chicken in a tub. Wicked.

I enjoyed Sundays in my neighborhood. It was quiet. Calm. All except for the street watch dog.

"Morning, Faryn." Interrupted. Cheryl, the neighbor from across the street took a few steps onto my front lawn. Her little excuse for a dog went to the end of his leash before squatting to piss on my grass. At the other end of the leash the morning sun flashed off Cheryl's rings. She wore at least one on every finger. Silver, gold, diamonds...did she just wear them all because she liked them or was she overcompensating for a husband that bought her guilt jewelry? Denial. Cheryl's teenaged son, Wendell, mowed my lawn and needed to make a visit. "Are you enjoying this surprise weather?" Was that a comment about my denim shorts and tank top while she wore an open winter coat? "Strange for Saskatchewan, eh?" It had been strangely warm for late autumn. "Did you hear the loud music last night? Somebody drove down the street with their music just blaring. They were having a party or something. Chow-Chow hid under the end table." Teehee.

The only thing I really got from that was, who names a dog Chow-Chow? "No, I was in most of the night watching a movie. My TV was loud." People didn't need to know what my life was like. I did hear the music, but I was naked in my tub with a plate of wings and getting high damn it. Let the city police handle it. If I did get dressed and go deal with it I probably would have said, fuck to being the good cop and asked them for a drink or a joint. The joy's of being single. Do what I want. Fuck who I want. Eat what I want, when I want, where I want. Smoke what I want. No need to worry about someone else's thoughts or what the white mutt was doing under the table. A nice Canadian lady leaning toward forty was not supposed to be that way, but who the hell ever said I was nice? Or a lady?

My nose twitched. I felt that familiar feeling. Ah. Ah. Here it came. Ah. Oh sweet release.

"Bless you."

And it was gone. Son of a bitch!

"I didn't see your lights on last night." Neighborhood Watch was trying to catch me in my immoral lie.

"Nope," was all I said.

Garth stopped singing as my phone started ringing. I saw the number. Chaos.

Chapter 2

THE CALL I GOT SAID, suicide by shotgun. Yuck. I hated investigating suicides. You never really knew what you were going to get when you pulled up. This one happened sometime over night in a field, so did the coyotes get to the body? How gross was it going to be? Then you had the often unanswerable questions. Would there really be answers to the why? Was there a reason for it all? Would anyone accept the reason? They always tended to be messy, both literally and actually.

There were too many suicides these days.

As a member of Major Crimes we went wherever we were needed in the province depending on the crime and area. Homicides, sexual assaults, robberies, attempted murders, threats and suspicious deaths. We got the gritty shit. The stuff worthy of TV dramas. "They are the members of the Major Crimes unit, and these are their stories" kind of shit. Da da.

Growing up I always thought the one place I never wanted to live was the province of Saskatchewan. It was a rectangle, trapezoid as Wendell pointed out once, with boring flat fields forever. Did you hear the one about the black dog that ran away in a Saskatchewan winter? We watched it for hours. Okay, a lot of the province was flat prairie, but in the north there was an area of sand dunes and a whole lot of thick forested area and lakes. In fact the province boasted one hundred thousand lakes. The central area changed to rolling hills. The crime scene was over an hour northeast of the city of Saskatoon through those rolling hills and fields.

I pulled my assigned Nissan Pathfinder SUV off to the side of a dirt road three cars behind the Mobile Command Post. The converted recreational camper was painted dark blue with all the Royal Canadian Mounted Police insignias. It kind of stuck out, along with the other police vehicles, on a grid road in the middle of harvested fields. The SUV, which was parked in front of the MCP, belonged to the Ident or Identification Unit. They were the crime scene techs who went over every single millimeter of the scene collecting possible evidence as they went. They had to deal with the physical mess while I was going to have to deal with the personal one.

Ahchoo! "Oh fuck yeah. Been waiting for that. Where's the body?" This area was classic central Saskatchewan. It was more flat than rolling. Harvested fields of tanned, almost grey stalks. There were spots of trees here and there and water holes called sloughs. They were dips in the earth where water collected after spring thaw and never seemed to go away. They were essential for wildlife, but hellish for farmers taking away some of the land which used to grow.

Constable Charles Delaney, of Major Crimes, looked up from where he was kneeling. In front of him was a black case he had just opened. "What? No pleasantries? No good morning, Chuck? How are you doing? Nice weather? What are your thoughts on the football game?"

A little growl escape my throat. I folded my hands behind my back and bent down to his level. Yes, I was fully aware that the ass hat was getting a view of my cleavage. What little I had was helped with one of Victoria's secrets. "Top of the morning to you, Charlie my bestest friend." Okay, my fake Irish accent sucked. "How are you doing on this fine autumn day?"

His eyes rolled as I stood back up. "I get it, Faryn, you're an ass."

"Like you should talk." I tied my mahogany hair back. Normally it fell to the top of my chest. "What the hell is that on your lip?"

He had to touch it as if he forgot. "It's Movember. Moustache plus November? You know what that is, right?"

"You look like you need to wash your face." Every November men across Canada grew facial hair to raise prostate cancer awareness. For most it meant a month long display of porn stashes. "Where's Brandi?"

He twitched his head to the side. "Follow the yellow flag road." He continued taking out the DJI Phantom 4 Pro drone. His baby. The four propeller driven drone would give us a birds eye view of the scene and area.

"We really need that for a suicide?"

This time Charlie didn't even look up at me. "We haven't found the victims car yet and it's a large search area. It's a wide open space with no other way to look except driving around." He glanced in my direction. "Seriously, is that what you wear to a crime scene?"

I dressed quickly after the musical interruption, but didn't think it that bad for a plain clothed officer. "What the fucks wrong with it? I thought every guy liked a woman in leggings."

"Not one with thunder thighs."

"What? Suck my dick!"

"Corporal Steel," Sergeant Jon Bisson's booming voice always made me catch my breath when he called my name. "In here." The tall man with broad shoulders, graying hair and year round moustache was up the back ramp to the command post. I stepped up nodding to Erik Saunders sitting in front of a computer. "Constable Saunders is going to be File Co-ordinator for this while you are head investigator. You're next up. I'll be Team Commander for this." Bisson was the commander of the Major Crimes unit, Saskatoon division. I felt the need to straighten my clothes out. Maybe Delaney was right. "Let's get this finished quickly."

We used a triangle, three point system, to investigate major crimes. The Team Commander, Bisson, was the top point. He would keep us on track, communicate with the higher ups, other departments and media. He controlled the flow of the investigation. As the FC, Saunders was another point on the triangle. He would collect all the information coming in from witness statements, to the drone photographs, to interviews and everything big and small dealing with the case. At the end, if need be, he would put it all into a neat little package for the lawyers, when and if a case ever went to court. I would make up the third point of the triangle. I was going to be doing the gumshoe work. This was what I got into policing for.

"A suicide shouldn't take long." I stepped into a white plastic suit and pulled it up over my body, tucking my hair inside the hood.

"Constable Faye has suspicions. Go talk to her."

Ident had a path marked with metal stakes and yellow flags. As they searched the earth this morning for footprints, garbage, particles, anything that could have been left by anyone they marked the path so they could safely move back and forth without tainting the scene. Once I had the bunny suit on, including slippers over my boots, I set down their path.

The field had been wheat which had been cut and harvested sometime over the last month. Wheat used to be the primary crop in Saskatchewan, but lentils, chick peas, dried peas and even mustard had become very important for the province. What remained in the field were short stiff cut-off stems of faded gold. The ground underneath was sticky mud threatening to pull the booties off. The field rolled over gentle hills. Halfway to where Ident had their large lights set up I walked past a dried slough with white cracked earth in it. This one was the size of an average pond. Off to the north was what was called Pelican Lake. I wasn't sure if it was a true lake or an oversized slough that never dried. It sounded like there were hundreds of geese around the lake squawking at each other as they prepared to fly south. The sound of autumn.

Death. I was breathing heavier by the time I came upon the body. The two Ident officers were on either side of it. Female. Caucasian. Her knees and lower legs were sticking out below the hem of a brown dress. Dried mud had been packed on her knees. Healthy body. I guessed she was about my height of 5'4. Maybe slightly smaller. A few extra pounds, though nothing to be upset about. Brunette? Her hair was so covered in her own blood that it was hard to definitively tell. Gunshot wound to the face. To me it looked like she had the barrel in her mouth or really close to her cheek and when she pulled the trigger it shot up and to the left taking half of her face. There was blood and flesh and bone and brain that blasted out from the left side of her head basically obliterating her physical identity. I couldn't even see where that eyeball was. The right side was against the ground.

This wasn't the first time I saw something like this and it wasn't even the worst. In the words of Patrick Swayze in the movie Roadhouse, it's amazing what you can get used to.

My attention fell on the 12 gauge Remington on the ground several feet away from the woman.

Her dress was chocolate brown, sleeveless with a halter neckline, the straps crossing over her chest, and fell to her knees. Not really my thing. There were no shoes on her feet which were also muddy. It had been warm for this time of year in Saskatchewan, however it was still chilly, maybe 10 degrees above freezing during the peak of day and below freezing at night. Either way she was not dressed for it. Even I was feeling the chill out in the open. This woman was dressed for a night out, probably in a city which was a long ways away. The City of Prince Albert was forty-five minutes away to the north and Saskatoon an hour in the other direction. Where did she come from?

"We haven't finished with the scene yet or really started on the body other than a cursory once over, so don't get any closer." Constable Brandi Faye was on her hands and knees studying the ground closely. "Don't step in any brain goop."

"Any identification?"

"No purse or wallet in the area, so nope." The last word made a pop noise. "We'll take her fingerprints and DNA samples, but you know that will only help if she has a criminal record."

"Not making this easy for us is she. Why kill yourself out in the middle of nowhere?"

"Here's something for you," Brandi stood and stretched her back. She was a bit shorter than myself. She had been in Ident for years and very little phased her. "I had a suspicion, so I measured from her face to her fingers, twenty-three inches. End of the gun barrel to trigger, thirty inches."

I wrote this down in my notebook. "So she's 7 inches short of shooting herself. That's a huge gap. Used a stick maybe?"

"Haven't found anything yet. Nothing within a ten foot radius anyway. It's not impossible, I guess."

The fact of it was that most women committed suicide with drugs, cutting themselves, drowning or hanging. They wanted things to be cleaner for those who were going to find them. Men were 3 times likelier to use a gun. This woman may not have committed suicide. I felt that suspicious tingling inside me.

"She also had multiple contusions on her, ah, still there face, bruising on the neck and arms. Looks like defensive wounds on her hands."

"You don't get that from shooting yourself so, ladies and gentlemen, we have ourselves a homicide."

"Seven?"

I gave Brandi a nod. She and her husband quizzed each other on movie trivia and we took it up. "She wasn't a professional."

"Why would you say that," Brandi asked.

I shrugged. "Just don't get that feeling. Never saw a hooker wear a dress like that. Not revealing enough. Was she sexually assaulted?"

"I took a look. It's a mess down there, Faryn. Bruising, contusions, blood. As far as I can tell she was brutalized. The coroner will have to give you the details. He's been called. I can say her panties, if she was wearing any, are not here."

"I don't often wear panties when I go out on a Saturday night."

Brandi glanced at the other Ident officer. "You and I lead two different lives."

"Where did she come from?" I turned in a complete circle and took in everything. Field to the north. Field to the East. Field to the South. Field to the West. Sure, there was the lake and roads in every direction, but they were all between a half and a kilometer away. The closest thing to the body was the road where the police vehicles were parked and even I found it a long hike in boots. There was a house, but that was a little farther across the field to the east.

"Still working on that. All we've found on the ground are dirt bike tire tracks and two pairs of small sneaker prints. Probably from the boys that found the body. And don't even ask about time of death. I would be making a guess. The coroner will give that after he looks at the body." Brandi looked at her partner again then turned back to me. "What did you do last night?"

"I had a bunch of rodeo clowns over and we played with my sex swing," I kept my gaze on the ground. There had to be something there.

Brandi's voice dropped. "You freak." That was because she knew I owned a sex swing. "Chicken wings in the tub, eh?" If the common person ever heard what cops talked about while standing over a dead body we would be branded just as heartless as the killer.

Chapter 3

AS I HEADED BACK TO the command post I wondered when the fields were harvested. How long could the body have stayed out there if it wasn't found? It was November and winter was coming. If snow fell the body may not have been found until spring when the fields were being prepped for planting. We were lucky she was found at all.

At a glance I couldn't tell the woman's age. I didn't have her name or her story. I didn't have much of anything. I was already behind.

"You're out of shape, Faryn." Charlie looked up for a moment from his tablet. I noticed the drone was gone.

"And you're ugly. At least I can get in shape." I stood beside him and tried looking at the tablet. Charlie towered a foot over me. "Where are the kids that found the body?"

"The house to the East of the scene. Someone is waiting for you there."

"Kay. Thanks."

"I found a car." He held the tablet high enough so that I couldn't see it. Asshole. "I have it going through to the monitor inside if you want."

Sgt. Bisson was gone. I stripped out of the bunny suit, placing it in a brown paper bag, and joined Erik Saunders at the computer. The monitor showed a birds eye view of fields and a dirt road. On it was a silver car sitting at an angle toward the ditch.

"Where is that?" I stared at the monitor.

"West. Over a kilometer away."

"I'm going. Send Ident. Call whoever's at the farmhouse and tell them to wait for me."

"Constable Garrett from the Wakaw detachment."

"Yeah, okay."

Dust rose behind the assigned SUV as I headed North to a connecting road. Rocks and dust spewed from the tires and bounced off the bottom under my seat. To get to the crime scene I turned off the highway at the hamlet of Domremy and then turned onto the dirt road where the MCP was. Saskatchewan was criss-crossed by a pattern of grid roads making property lines between the fields. Not many were passable in the winter because they were never plowed. Soon half of these just wouldn't exist for a few months. Once you got away from the highways houses were spread out. I did not pass a single home before turning.

Something grabbed the tires. The dirt went darker as if it had been raining all morning. The earth pulled the front end of the vehicle to the side. I yanked the wheel the other way. In front of me tires had sunk into the same ground. Ahead of me was a silver car pulled off to the side of the road at a sharp angle. Its tail end was out toward the middle. Mud had been shot out as its tires spun. The sunken tire tracks were obviously the cars. It had swerved back and forth across the road, even going sideways, before stopping where it was. My own car suddenly turned to the far side. The tires spun up mud as my hands rapidly turned the steering wheel. I heard the wet slap of damp dirt against the walls. They whined. My arms muscled the steering wheel to the left. The SUV bounced from the road into the field on the far side before I stepped on the brakes. I was lucky there were no deep ditches here like where I was from. In most cases the roads just seemed like they were cut through the fields with the only changes being one was dirt and the other had things growing in it.

My breath came fast. My knuckles were white on the steering wheel. Why was the road muddy and slick when all others were dry? There had been a little rain over the past few days, but not enough to swamp out one section of road. That might have been why the victim was on foot. The police vehicle had all wheel traction. The car didn't.

I radioed the road conditions to the others before stepping from my car. The grass on the edge of the road was dry and brittle. Given binoculars I might be able to see the crime scene from here. The victims car had mud splattered behind the front wheels. It travelled up the doors to the windows.

As I stepped onto the road the soil wanted to suck my boots off my feet. There was a smell. Tainted. I had to balance myself as I slipped across the road trying hard not to pull my feet right out of my heavy boots.

I shielded my eyes as I peered into the car windows. Her panties were on the back seat. Black. Lacy. The kind you wear when you go out hoping to hook up. Did she know the guy she was wearing them for? Assumptions. Already I felt like eliminating half the population due to one item. There were food containers on the floor, but not much else out in the open. I scanned the road and saw no tire tracks over hers except for my own. There were footprints in the mud right outside the drivers door. She slipped and fell before heading towards where the body was found. This was where her knees got packed with mud. There was nothing to tell about what type of shoes she had on. There were holes in the ground, possibly from a high heel. The passenger door was over the hard field, so if anyone got out that way they probably wouldn't have left prints. Maybe she could see the light from the house and that was where she was running to. A lot of properties had huge lights on tall poles to keep the coyotes away at night.

I returned to the SUV for yellow police tape from the back. Using sticks I secured a barrier as best I could around the car and prints. I noted the license plate and vehicle identification number before heading on my way. I drove in the field as far as I could before getting back on the road.

Chapter 4

"CALCIUM CHLORIDE," Constable Paige Garrett said as I stepped from the SUV in front of the house closest to the scene. My boots were still caked in the stuff. It had sprayed up the white sides of the vehicle. "Farmer's spray it on the roads to keep the dust down. When it gets a little wet it becomes a mud slick like a quicksand road. You okay?" She wore the navy blue tactical uniform with a reflective stripe the length of each leg.

"I should be asking you that." Three dogs barked at us from a fenced area at the back of the house where there was also a light on the top of a huge pole.

Paige was chewing on her lip like it was gum. She wiped at a tear before it could fall and smudged her mascara. She shrugged her shoulders. "I'm holding it together. It's personal shit more than this."

"Well, be all business for now. We'll talk about other stuff later. This is where the teens that found the body are?" I looked in the direction where the body would be. The house and barn were all surrounded by tall spruce except for the driveway that continued through the yard and into the field through an opening in the wind break. I could barely see where Ident had their equipment set up.

Paige took a breath. "Yes, twin boys Andy and Zeke Thompson-Bing, eleven years old, went in the field on dirt bikes around 8am and came across the body. They told their mom who went out there to double check. She got as close as she wanted and then called the police."

Both boys were blond with the clean faces of the prepubescent. Both sat on chairs in front of a big screen television. One was playing the video game Red Dead Redemption.

"We were racing to the lake when we saw her," Andy said.

"Mom called the police," Zeke didn't even look away from fighting zombies on horseback.

Their mother stood in the kitchen near a sink of dirty dishes. She too was blond and had scars on her cheeks where she had had acne at one time.

"Do you own the fields back there?" I looked out the kitchen window. The fields were blocked by hanging plants.

"No." The mother looked a little green. "They are owned by the Gaudet family. We don't farm. My husband is a plumber. Gardening, that's about all the farming we do here." I had noticed bare dirt where the garden had been.

"Did you notice anything happening in the field last night or yesterday? Hear any sounds? Any gun shots?"

"It's hunting season. There's always gun shots, but no, I haven't heard anything recently. I try to stop the boys from riding in the fields chasing the birds, but they insist they are safe with their orange vests on."

"We went in the field yesterday," one of the boys said.

The other added, "the body wasn't there."

I turned back to the wife. "Where is your husband?"

"He left at 4am for Regina with his friends. It's a big football weekend." Her gaze bounced around the room. The Saskatchewan Roughriders played in Regina and they were in the running for the Grey Cup. "I can give you his phone number."

"Thank you." I wrote a few notes including her husbands phone number. "One last thing, Mrs. Thompson-Bing, do you have any guns in the house?"

"No, of course not. David has talked about getting one for coyotes but I keep saying no. The boys are crazy enough without weapons."

"Thank you for your help. We can let ourselves out." At the door we stopped to put our boots back on. I looked up to see the boys watching us. One had a cell phone in his hand. "I better not see any pictures of the body on Facebook or Instagram. That's illegal, you know." At one time an old boyfriend said my rough voice was deep and earthy. It was rough enough to make the twins eyes blow up wide.

"How is the investigation going?" The irises of Paige's eyes were green with a blue ring around the outside like Saturn's rings. This morning they had red lines on the white and looked tired.

"Lots of questions, no answers." I hoped for something better, though I knew it would probably only get worse.

Chapter 5

RUNNING A VEHICLE'S license plate and VIN usually worked a lot faster than fingerprints and DNA. Those had to be sent to a lab, run through tests, reports written and sent back to us before we could determine what was what. Even then if somebody was not in the database you were left with nothing. It could take over a week to get back a report saying, yes, we are able to obtain a DNA profile, but no, we have no clue who they are. Real life was nothing like television crime dramas where with the spin of a centrifuge they knew everything about the victim. For the vehicle information it was as simple as typing. Type, type, enter, results. In this case I called in both identification numbers and let someone else type.

The license plate and car VIN did not go together. The license plate belonged to a Douglas Bloom in a city 500 kilometers away and the car was registered to a Marly Hudson who lived in Saskatoon. I quickly pointed the SUV south and headed back to the city. Was this our victim and why did she have someone else's license plate? More questions.

The long drive gave me time to go over the questions I needed to answer. I thought about the body and her obliterated face. Did someone not like her? Did she witness something? It seemed personal. Did someone just brutalize her randomly or was she targeted? Wrong place? Wrong time.? Gangs were an issue in Saskatchewan. Yes. Street gangs in the prairie, believe it or not. They took whatever they wanted and destroyed the rest. This didn't look like their thing, however, and they didn't venture out into the rural areas much. Was there a random psycho out there?

By the time I got back to Saskatoon I got a call that constables in Regina visited eighty-two year old Douglas Bloom. They said he pulled an oxygen tank with him when he came to the door, so he wasn't much of a suspect. He didn't know his license plate was even stolen. His car was parked in his driveway and he couldn't recall the last time he drove it. In the province of Saskatchewan you only had to have plates on the back of the car and his car was parked facing his house, so he never walked around to the back of it. The plate could have been taken weeks before.

After stopping to do a quick clothing change, grey slacks, matching blazer and black blouse, I rang the doorbell to the house I was sent to.

Marly Hudson's vehicle registration said she lived there and that she was twenty years old. The house had a metal frame fence around a front yard that looked untouched except by a lawn mower, occasionally, and a garage at the end of an asphalt driveway. I grew up in the country where there was one door in the front of the house and one in the back. I hated city homes that had a door facing the street and another just around the side. They both opened to the same area, but one was NEVER used. Which one did you go to? I picked the door with nothing on the stairs.

Was this girl going to be my victim or was the car going to be as stolen as the license plate?

The woman that opened the door had to be in her sixties. She stared at me with no signs of wanting to speak. "Hi. I'm Corporal Faryn Steel of the RCMP. Does Marly Hudson live here?"

"I'm her mother, Sheila. What has she done? What's happened?" Her eyes doubled in size. Her body began to shake. She was a woman expecting the worst.

I flashed her a half smile to try and calm her down. "She's done nothing that I know of. Her car was found at a scene this morning and we're just trying to figure out what it was doing there. The license plate was stolen, so the car might have been as well. Could I speak to her?" I could have told her about the body, but at the moment we knew nothing about the victim.

"She doesn't live here anymore. She hasn't for about seven months." Sheila's white hair was puffed out. Her shoulders were slouched forward. She looked like a woman who was tired.

Damn. "Where can I find her?"

A kettle whistle went off somewhere inside the house. The woman turned around and headed toward the sound without a word to me. As a second thought she glanced back and invited me in. "Keep your shoes on if you want."

The front door opened to a sort of boot area. I looked to my right and saw the other front door with garbage cans blocking it. The rest of the room was an open concept living room and kitchen. I could see how clean it was, so I took my boots off. There was a television in the corner. Drew Carey asked if the price was right. A man, also in his sixties or older sat in a lounger with a newspaper open on his lap that he wasn't looking at. There were pictures on the walls of a girl seen every year through school photographs. She appeared mousey looking. Washed out. Blond hair, blue eyes, pale skin. Smile, happy, happy, barely a grin, frown, looking down right pissed off. Something changed in her life. The last one showed her wearing a graduation cap and gown. At least she had a smile in that one, even if it looked fake. There were trophies amongst ceramic dolphins and more framed photos on every ledge. In the family pictures the girl wasn't smiling. On the back of the couch was one of those crocheted squares blankets that my mother had made once. It was a cozy place, but not one for a young woman.

My mother "made" the blanket was an exaggeration. Started and paid someone to finish was the way it was. Her house was the same as this one with the fake smiles in pictures and trophies in the corner. Fake praise for a daughter she didn't care about. Was that the way it was here?

"Would you turn that down," Sheila snapped at her husband. The woman walked toward him instead of the kitchen, grabbed the television remote and turned the volume down herself before heading toward the kettle whistle. He muttered a few profanities, but didn't turn it back up.

"Sorry, Hank is hard of hearing, so the TV is turned up so loud it's making me hard of hearing. Would you like some tea?"

"No thank you. Can we talk about Marly? What's she like?" As long as the blond girl on the wall was Marly it was a good sign that she wasn't the dead woman from this morning, however hair colour could always be changed. I slid onto a chair at the table.

"She is quiet. Always keeps to herself. She would come home and go right to her room. Most days I only saw her for supper." She stared into her cup as she stirred. "She used to be outgoing and excited about everything. She always wanted to play. Then she just got quiet. Teenagers." She sat down at the dining table with both hands around her China cup. "Hank retired two years ago. That's when Marly really got quiet. I guess we weren't fun anymore. I retired last year. A young woman didn't want to be in the house with two old timers all the time."

"You said she left seven months ago? Why did she leave?"

"She was coming home drunk and seeing boys. She had to argue about everything." Hank Hudson crossed to the refrigerator, took out a beer and twisted the cap off. His back was bent. His fingers were thick. "She wasn't our girl anymore. One day quiet, next day angry, never happy. That wasn't our girl." He took a drink. A drop fell from his lip.

"I thought you were hard of hearing."

"That's what Marly thought too, but if I turn up my hearing aid I can hear a pin drop down the hall. She didn't think I heard her talking to her boyfriend about taking money from us and moving in with him after knowing him only a few weeks. I told her I wasn't leaving and if she didn't like my rules then she could leave." He took a long drink. He wasn't as weak as he seemed.

"Do you know the boyfriend name?"

Hank growled, ignoring the question, and returned to his chair. He sat down and turned the television volume back up.

Sheila took a sip of her tea before speaking. She had changed during our conversation. Her face seemed grayer, if that was possible. "I think his name was Vincent. I don't recall her telling me his last name. She said he worked at the lumber yard in the Rona store on Albert street. We didn't know what to do. She could get so angry sometimes. She would blow up and throw things. Then I got really worried with how suddenly quiet and lonely she could become."

"Have you spoken to her since she left?"

"She called a couple of times over the first month after she left, but nothing since then. I'm hoping she comes home for Christmas. When I've called her cell phone I get a message saying it's out of service."

I wrote down the number she said wasn't working anymore. "You never reported her missing?"

Sheila glanced at her husband. "She is a twenty year old. I never thought of her as missing. Kids move out. If you find her will you tell her to come home for Christmas?"

Chapter 6

I HAD MY CELL PHONE in my hand and a pre-set number pushed before I even got off their deck. By the time I was in my car it was answered. "It's me. Do we have a time of death yet?"

"You know I'm still at the scene right?" Brandi sounded annoyed that I even called. "Coroner says likely between midnight and 6 am. That was the best he could say until the autopsy tomorrow."

"Still no ID?" I knew if they had found one I would have been the first person called.

"Not yet."

"Okay. I'm going to keep chasing down the owner of the car. I'll call you later." The only lead I had on the car was that the owners boyfriend had worked at a Rona hardware store seven months ago. I've followed weaker leads before.

I had to go through the lumber manager, the assistant store manager and the store manager before getting the name Vincent Jones and an address.

"Vincent Jones?" I stared at the man who opened the third floor apartment door. He looked fit, in his twenties, scruff on his face and messy hair as if he just woken up. He nodded and I introduced myself. "Is Marly Hudson here?"

"Marly?" He glanced behind himself. "I haven't seen her in months. Why would she be here?"

"Her vehicle was found at a crime scene this morning and we are trying to find out why it was there. Do you know where I can find Marly?"

"A crime scene? What kind of crime? Is she okay? What happened to her?" Already he cared more than her own parents seemed to.

"How long were you seeing Marly?"

"Like a few weeks. We weren't like boyfriend and girlfriend. We would hang out and mess around. Shit like that."

"Vince? What is this?" A woman walked up behind him. She had black hair and a pretty face except for the crooked teeth that seemed out of place. Her belly pushed out against a t-shirt in that round pregnant way.

Vincent took her hand. "She's a detective. She's looking for Marly. Like I said, I haven't talked to Marly in about six months or so. I met Julie around the same time we split."

I nodded toward the woman's belly. "How far along are you?"

"Six months."

"Congratulations. Is this why you split with Marly?" This would certainly account for some of the anger before she left home if the relationship was sour.

"What? No, after. I met Julie like a week or so after I last saw Marly and we really hit it off. Marly had been talking about some guy who was giving her a new, what did she call it, outlook. Some guy named Pony. I don't know what was going on, but it sounded like a lot more than a new outlook. I met Julie right away so I didn't care about it. Talk to Heather. She's Marly's best friend. I think I have her number."

"Yes, I'm Heather Marquand. I haven't talked to Marly in months. We were best friends all through school and high school then I went into college and she didn't, so we didn't talk as much and started to drift apart, I guess. We went to parties sometimes. It happens, right?"

I stared across the table at the woman with long bottle red hair. I had found her at the college. "So, you don't know where I can find her?"

"No, I haven't seen her in a while."

"Do you know if she still has her car?" I had come to the realization that Marly, at the present moment, was my only suspect and possible victim. Her mother had let me take a picture of the most recent photograph which was still over a year old, however. I didn't know who my victim was, I didn't know who my suspect was. I didn't know much of anything.

Heather shrugged. "I guess so. I don't know. Last time I talked to her she was getting rid of her possessions, so maybe not."

"Why would she be getting rid of her possessions?"

Heather gathered her books together. "She just was. She had become sad and quiet until she met Randall Pony and then she seemed happier, but she also didn't want to be around any of us. She was fighting with her family and just seemed to go away inside, you know. The last time I heard from her she was asking to borrow money."

As she got up to leave I asked who Randall Pony was.

"I don't know. I never met him. I just remember her saying the name when she showed me a brochure for this place called the Stable. I think she called him Pony more than using his first name. When I asked about him she got defensive, so I stopped asking and after that we stopped really talking."

I wrote down the man's name and the "Stable." Barn? Farm?

"Any idea why her car would be in Domremy?"

"That's where the Stable was. She said it was a place to enjoy nature and get centered. I never heard her talk about this new age stuff before and I wasn't into it. I just remember the name because I ride horses and that's what I thought it was at first."

Chapter 7

THE SHEER NUMBER OF police dramas that have ever been on television was staggering and each one seemed to help damage people's perceptions on actual police investigations. People believed that everything could be packed into a short time frame. Talk to victim – don don – talk to suspect – don don – talk to another suspect – don don – interrogation, teary admission of guilt, trial, done. On the shows the investigations seemed to last a few days. Bad guy caught, victim vindicated, let's have pie. On one show, that worked heavily with the science, they got reports in seconds that in the real world could take days or weeks, even months. Real victims families got frustrated because things were supposed to be like on TV. Sorry. We moved at real speed. It took time to find a person and get to where they were. It took time to find the owner of an abandoned car. Here I was past mid-day with still no identification of the body and I couldn't even find the owner of the fucking vehicle found close to the scene and I didn't even know if it had anything to do with the death anyway.

I drove out of the city and headed Northeast on highway 41. I wanted to find Marly Hudson. There was always a reason for people to become suddenly withdrawn and quiet. It usually wasn't good. For me it was one of my mother's boyfriends wanting to get too close and me not being able to fight back or my mother not wanting to listen. I wanted to find Marly, if only to make sure she was okay.

A quick search online for the Stable came up with a definition, three horse ranches, and a wellness center just north of Wakaw. Their claims were that they helped with addictions by natural healing. The description was extremely vague, but fit what I was told about where Marly went.

Saskatchewan towns were originally along the railroad tracks. Whatever was farmed went in all directions and across the oceans. When highways were built and wheels took over for tracks many towns and hamlets vanished with the dust. There were over one hundred ghost towns in the province because of things like the TransCanada Highway.

Wakaw was one of the small towns that was not thriving, but wasn't shrinking. It was at the crossroads of two highways and was next to popular summer lakes. People from the city came out there every summer to their camps and to support the town's economy. It had a Dairy Queen, Subway, Chinese restaurant, hardware store, a roadside motel with continental breakfast and two grocery stores. During the summer and the holiday season a passenger train ran from Wakaw to Cudworth and back, about a twenty minute trip one way, with onboard entertainment and a dinner or lunch at the end.

Before I got to the Wakaw turn one of our computer analysts called with information on Pony.

"Randall Poniatowski, aka Randall Pony, aka Pony. He has trafficking and assault charges from eight years ago. The assault was on a woman. Time served. Thirty-two years of age, 5'9, 168 pounds, brown hair, hazel eyes."

"Thanks, Jon. Can you pass that onto Saunders and have him get Ident to cross any fingerprints."

"Already done. I've sent you the file and his picture."

"You're the best." I turned off the highway into Wakaw. "Continue with the missing person reports. Contact Saskatoon police and Prince Albert police. See what they have."

Chapter 8

"PONY. SOUNDS LIKE he's over compensating for something. Yeah, I'm Pony. I've got a huge horse cock." My mocking voice needed work. From my experience men who bragged were full of shit.

"He's not that bad." Paige Garrett sat in my passenger seat. I picked her up at the Wakaw detachment to act as my escort since she knew the area and people. "I've been there on a couple disturbance calls. The farm across the road reported screaming or people running around. Upon responding we were told it was a therapy technique. Primal scream therapy thingy. I don't get it myself, but there was nothing illegal about it. They advertise it as a non-traditional addiction recovery facility, whatever that means."

Paige was pretty. Pointed chin, bubble gum lips, curved eyebrows and Mila Kunis eyes. She probably didn't even know how pretty she was. "So what had you so upset this morning?"

She took a breath. "The guy I'm seeing. It's stupid to bring it to work, I know. And then the body just, I don't know."

"Not all of us can be cold hearted bitches and leave it at the door like people say I am. I'm not. I go to Studio Fitness before most people are awake and I leave my life problems on a punching bag there."

"Turn here."

As I turned the Pathfinder I caught a glimpse of her looking my way. "What? Okay, I am a cold hearted bitch. Ask any guy I've ever dated. The job comes first and men are disposable." I had to laugh at her wide eyes. "Not everyone has to be like me."

"Are you dating anyone now?"

"Dating anyone? No, I'm not. I don't like to stick to convention."

"What does that mean? The driveway on the right. See that sign?"

I forgot about her question.

There were harvested fields in all directions and with patches of trees. Around the Stable property were perfectly lined pines making two rows around the entire acreage with large leafy trees between the rows, most of the leaves had fallen, making an almost solid wind barrier. There was a sign of stained wood at the end with carved letters and a burnt frame that read The Stable. That was it. Not a word about what they were. Pony. The Stable. I couldn't help but snicker. The trees on both sides of the driveway turned inward making a shoot of towering evergreens. One side of the driveway had an elaborate flowerbed, the flowers gone and the earth dug up, with smooth rocks around a drained pond. The rocks stacked like a mountain were a fountain when it was running. The grass was well kept. As we got to the end of the trees a two story house came into view to the right. It had a two car garage and a deck that sat on one side and wrapped around to the back. Next to this was a yard with fruit trees and bushes. Inside I could see the tree barrier made a perfect square around the property. There was a blue sided barn with roof shingles that curled up, and a few more out buildings. Behind them I saw a large garden. A few people were moving about and looked up at the sound of an engine. I parked behind an old yellow Volkswagen Beetle. There was also a Ford pickup and a silver Honda Civic. As our vehicle came to a stop a man looked out from behind the Beetle.

"How close are we to the crime scene?" There was a man with a crew cut in a camouflage jacket pushing a wheelbarrow, another man was walking away with a chainsaw. Two women in jean jackets glanced at us then back to their work.

Paige sucked her lip as she thought. "About eight kilometers. Maybe more."

Close enough.

"That's him," Paige nodded. "That's Pony."

He watched us with intense eyes from behind the Volkswagen. At first he probably thought we were new lost souls, but there was a change in his gaze when he saw Paige and her uniform. He wore dirty denim jeans and a T-shirt with a half buttoned flannel over top. He ran a hand through sandy hair that fell to his jaw line and adjusted his round glasses. For a moment when he saw us his lips turned down and then he waved and smiled.

"Make sure you get those license plate numbers," I said to Paige as she was about to open her door.

I scanned the yard as I stepped from the SUV. Except for the fact that there were over a half dozen adults around doing different jobs it looked like any other homestead. I buttoned my blazer.

"Hey, Pony, do you remember me? Constable Garrett with the RCMP?"

"Yes, of course. Beautiful day, isn't it?"

Paige ignored the question. "This is Corporal Steel."

"Steel? Strong name for a cop. How can I help you, Officer?" He only looked at Paige for a moment before facing me. He wiped his hands on a rag. They had very little grease on them to begin with.

"I prefer Corporal over Officer, please." I kept my voice flat but firm. I wasn't sure what I was dealing with yet.

Pony smiled. He had acne on his chin and by one sideburn. He looked younger than his age. "Sorry about that. Say, wasn't there a famous Steel with the RCMP?"

"Sam Steele, but he was with the North-West Mounted Police, which the RCMP became, and it's a different spelling. No relation. Do you mind if we talk to you for a minute, Mr. Poniatowski?" To tell the truth, I had been practicing his last name in my head for over 10 minutes during the drive so I would get it right.

His lips tightened together and his eyes focused on me for a moment before they softened again. Intensity. "Call me Pony. Here at The Stable everyone gets a name that either comes from their name, like Pony, or comes from their personality or what they are looking for."

"So what is this place exactly?"

"It's many things to many people," his arms opened wide. "In the basic form it is a voluntary, full lifestyle rechargement. People come here to get away from the trials of society for a time and give up their addictions. Recharge their soul battery if you will."

"Are you a psychologist?" A blond woman rubbernecked from behind the Volkswagen. She looked very familiar.

Pony sighed. "No, I'm not. Everyone that comes here knows that. This is just a place for them to heal themselves. I was a licensed therapist and an addictions counselor, but I gave that up. I'm willing to listen. I don't tell anyone who comes here that they will be healed or their lives fixed or anything like that. They come here for as little or as long as they like. No cell phones, television, computer access or any significant communication with their old lives. And I see by the look on your face that you have the question everyone has on their minds. No, they don't pay me anything. They live here, work the land, work the animals. We sell our wares at farmers markets. Some people do arts and crafts or use whatever talents they have to offer. We all work together for each other. Others also come here just during the day and help with what they can before returning to their lives."

"How many people are here?"

"Right now, eight of us are here. We've had as many as thirteen living here at one time. We all live and work together. Everyone is free to come and go, but the program works best if they stay for a period of time."

For what seemed like a long moment the two of us gazed into each others eyes. His whole philosophy of the Stable did not sound legit, but that wasn't what we were there for. It was too easy. There was something behind it he wasn't telling me. "Do you know a Marly Hudson?"

He flipped his hair back from his face. "Of course. We don't refer to her as that here. Here she has completely submerged herself in our philosophy and has been reborn again. That's why we named her Phoenix. Phoenix, come here please."

The blond woman behind the yellow Volkswagen walked around to stand beside him. She wore jeans and a hooded sweatshirt with a faded logo. She wore no makeup and looked a little washed out. Grey even. Her hair was longer than the picture I got from her mother, but this was Marly Hudson. Her face looked relaxed. Calm.

"Marly Hudson?" She nodded. "I'm Corporal Faryn Steel. Your mother is really worried about you."

The young woman's arms hugged her own body. "If you see her again let her know I'm, like, fine. I'm happy." All it took was a smile and I would have believed her, maybe. Nope.

"I will. It would be better coming from you though. Do you own a car, Miss Hudson? A 2015 silver Dodge Neon?"

"My name is Phoenix now. I did own a car. I don't have it anymore." Her voice wasn't as robotic as her words made it seem. She wasn't as confident as she wanted to be, but she was trying. Was that part of the Pony method?

"Where is it?"

She looked at Pony.

"It was stolen," he said. "I think it was three weeks ago in Saskatoon. We had gone into the city that weekend to the farmers market and when we left at the end of the day it was gone. Coyote had to come pick us up."

"Did you report it to the police?" Paige asked. She had been pacing behind me, but within ear shot.

Pony put his hand behind Marly's back, but I could tell he was not touching her. "No, we didn't. Whoever took the car obviously needed it more than we did and here we believe things are meant to be."

"You have no idea who took it?"

"None at all."

Marly shook her head.

"To be honest, the insurance had lapsed and we shouldn't have been using it anyway," Pony said. "We took the car being stolen as a sign."

"Any idea why it had a different license plate?"

"What?"

"It had a license plate stolen from a vehicle in Regina." I kept my gaze on both of them. Marly rubbed her arms. Pony barely moved.

"Why are you asking about the car, Officer ... Corporal?" Pony's voice had stayed calm through the entire conversation. He reminded me of the boys in high school that were too cool to be there. Matthew McConaughey from the movie Dazed and Confused. The cool philosopher. He wasn't someone who would be charged with assault. At least that was the personality he was putting forward.

"It was found this morning at a crime scene eight kilometers from here. It seems a little strange that your car, Marly, was stolen -"

"I said my name is Phoenix!"

"- a week ago, but then ended up just a few kilometers away with a stolen license plate." I looked from the young woman to the man beside her. He stared back at me with a calm expression. "It seems almost impossible that someone would steal it a week ago and then abandon it so close to where you live."

"I don't know what to tell you, Officer," that was Pony's way of saying he could play the game. "We haven't seen the car since we got to the farmers market. And it was three weeks ago it was stolen, not one. That it was near here is a coincidence. Maybe it was fates way to get you here. What kind of demons do you have?"

I wasn't going to take him there. "Where were you last night?" I held Pony's gaze with my own. There were no twitches or eye movements that signaled anything. He would have been excellent on the poker circuit.

"Seriously? What time?"

I let a breath out. "All night."

Pony looked at both police officers. "We had supper around six. After that we had a discussion circle that ended around nine o'clock. After that everyone settled down. A couple of us went for a drive. We came back around midnight and went to bed."

"Where did you go," Paige asked.

Pony looked at her in silence for a moment. "Just around. There are a lot of dirt roads around here. I didn't see anything if that's going to be your next question. I'm sure the others didn't either."

"It wasn't. What about everyone else? Where were they?"

"Here. They can each vouch for each other. They need to get permission from me before leaving and nobody requested it. Before you ask, I trust these people. They follow the rules. We all help each other to keep the bad out and embrace the new life."

I didn't reply to that one. His statement was sketchy at best. The whole place seemed out of whack, but without any evidence I wouldn't get anywhere. I thought about what the young woman's parents said about her change. "Marly, could I speak to you alone for a moment?" She didn't respond. "Phoenix, sorry. Please?" I started walking away without an answer. She followed. We walked far enough that the others could still hear but they weren't right on top of us. I kept her back to Pony. "I was talking to your parents earlier and they told me your personality changed a while ago. You went from a happy playful person to being quiet and wanting to be alone. I'm curious about what happened to make that change. Do you feel like telling me?" My eyes flicked and I saw Pony watching us. His eyes on me was not uncomfortable.

"Nothing happened. I'm fine." As a woman I knew what the word, fine, meant.

"Okay. Here is my card. It has all my numbers on it. Call me if you ever want to talk about anything. You guys do have phones right?" I thought it was a joke. In this day and age everyone had a phone.

"There's one in the house," she said before taking my business card and putting it in her jacket pocket and briskly walking away. She surveyed the ground. I stared at Pony who stared back.

Chapter 9

BACK ON THE ROAD PAIGE asked me what I thought. I looked vacantly out the windshield at the fields and trees and whatever else was there to look at. When I was a kid on road trips with my grandparents I stared out the side window and would imagine myself running beside the car, leaping over driveways and rivers. Now I just looked for things out of place. Occupational hazard. I didn't see the world anymore like I used to. "I was hoping I would take a step forward, but I took one back. My only real clue is a dead end. We're no further along than when we first saw the body."

"What do you think of Pony?"

"I don't believe him. I don't think he lied about everything, but he did about something. I just don't know what about." I glanced at Paige who was staring back at me. "I have nothing to connect him or anyone else to the crime or scene, but I don't believe in coincidence."

"What do you believe in then?"

I didn't have to think about that one. "Fact. I believe in what can be proved. I believe in guilty or not guilty and I believe there are one hundred shades of grey in between. It's our job to put a light on it all. What I don't believe in is coincidence." I didn't want to say it, but Pony bugged me. I couldn't say if he had anything to do with the dead girl in the field. Just something about him made me want to go back and question him more. Maybe search the Stable or talk to everyone there. If all that he said about what they did was true then it was a good place. I really didn't want to believe him.

"Nice working with you, Corporal," Paige said. She opened the passenger door at the Wakaw depot.

"You can call me Faryn when we're alone, Paige. You did good. You asked questions when you felt a silence and stayed quiet when you had to be. If I need your help again I know where to find you. And you have my number if anything comes up."

I headed back to the city. Hopefully there was something in missing persons.

Chapter 10

"WHAT ARE YOU SMILING about?" Constable Erik Saunders handed me my bulldog mug.

I looked up from my cell phone and quickly put it in my pocket. "I wasn't smiling." Caught.

"Yes you were. You were looking at your phone and smiling like you had a secret."

Charlie stopped as he was walking by. "Get a text from your guy? Who is he? Was it a dick pic?"

"No! Don't you have shit to do, Chucky?" I poured my coffee. Some things were meant to stay private. My life outside of the job was different and most people wouldn't understand.

"Why so private, Faryn? You have something to hide?" His moustache made it look like he had crap on his teeth when he smiled. Again I got the urge to hit him. Erik was at least trying to pretend like he wasn't interested.

"It was a text from my old friend Jimmy." No it wasn't. "He's a country singer out west in Middleton. Can I get back to work now?"

"What's his last name?"

"You're an investigator, Chuck. Investigate." My desk was close to the middle of the room. To everyone else my desk top looked messy. I knew where everything was. Right.

"This guy ever write a song about you?" Yes.

I put my mug down, slipped into my chair and let my head fall back. "I'm like eight hours into this and I don't even have an ID on my victim yet. Leave me alone."

"That's not a no." Charlie swayed as he walked away.

As everyone who has seen a crime drama knows, the first forty-eight hours of an investigation were the most important and there were steps to follow. Identify victim. Collect evidence. Identify persons of interest. Build a case. We had no identification, there was some evidence and, yeah, next.

"Check your email," Erik sipped his coffee as he leaned a hip against my desk. "The analysts sent some missing persons reports to look at. There wasn't much to go on."

The missing person reports were all going on the premise that Jane Doe was missing. If she just went out last night and ran into her killer then her family and friends may not have known she was gone yet. There were three files attached to the email.

My computer binged indicating a new email. I opened it and read a little before mentioning it to Erik. "Preliminary Autopsy report is in. Victim is in her twenties. We already knew. Blood tested positive for alcohol. Evidence of past knee surgery on her left knee. Maybe we can use that to identify her. Signs of sexual trauma. Believed to have been assaulted with a foreign object. Ejaculate found and sent for DNA testing." The DNA, if there was any in the sample, would be tested against samples in the National DNA database for any connections to other crimes. Unfortunately most of the samples in there were collected from conviction of a sexual offense or similar violent crime. If whoever did this wasn't convicted at any time his sample would not be on file. It was like a puzzle my mother had. All of the pieces were the same shape and size, double sided with almost the same picture on the back as on the front. We had all the pieces but the design wasn't matching. "She will be doing the full autopsy first thing in the morning."

A third email sat in my inbox with photographs of the Jane Doe and scene. I got to the close-ups of her body parts. Her one eye that remained was brown with gold flakes. Her hair was indeed brown with some highlights. She had freckles on her cheek. There were also pictures of her hands showing that she had a manicure. A pedicure too. Someone just going through life and then half her face was gone. As usual I wondered if I should worry about myself for not being affected by what was on the screen. Erik wasn't looking.

"I don't think she was a hooker," I said more to the little voice in my head than anyone else, "the dress, the mani-pedi, the hair. She cared about herself and her appearance. She took the time. She had probably gone out looking for a good night. A safe night." I imagined her at a bar. All the people in the room were having a good time. There were drinks and music and dancing. She had to build up her courage to talk to some guy. And somewhere amongst the crowd a pair of eyes were gleaming in the dim light. Staring at her. Hunting her. Or was it someone she trusted? Someone plotting? "This definitely wasn't accidental."

People vanished without a trace all the time. The common person sitting in their homes watching Law & Order and Criminal Minds snorted at their flat screens unconvinced as to how people could disappear off the face of the earth. We saw it all too much. There one day then swallowed up the next. Working in northern communities we saw it happen too often. Women just stepped off the earth and barely a sound bite was recorded. The search continues for blah blah. The Prime minister announces his water box drink like containers and the lost woman is forgotten. I couldn't have this woman be a lost statistic.

My mother disappeared. The only excuse I ever got out of her was that she couldn't deal with things. A couple of times she just didn't come home. Sometimes she would come back a couple days later. A few times she was gone for weeks and once I didn't know if she was ever coming back. She did, with a fiancé and a baby in her belly. Like always it was as if she never left. She complained about the milk being sour and there being no food in the house. I was a teenager. I got an after school job just to keep myself alive. Dad had left her after her missing episodes started when I was twelve because he couldn't handle her anymore and he thought she would be responsible if he wasn't there to be her crutch, so I guess it wasn't as big a thing as it could have been. I hated her for being who she was and hated him for leaving me there. He may have not been able to take it, but I didn't know how to handle taking care of my brother and sister and mother. There was never a missing persons report done on her.

Chapter 11

"READ THE NEXT ONE."

Brandi hummed before starting. "Jordann Avery. Reported missing four months ago by her mother. Twenty-three, 5'6, long brown hair, brown eyes, no tattoos, scar on her left knee from surgery at the age of sixteen. Missing four months from the East side of S'toon. You really think this could be our Jane Doe?"

I glanced at Constable Brandi Faye in the passenger seat. She was dressed in the dark blue tactical uniform that had hundreds of pockets. She didn't have as much tactical gear on her belt as a regular officer would have. It was more for her actual tasks. Her amber hair was cut short above her shoulders. It suited her long thin face. "It's what I have right now. The knee scar fits. Everything else is possible. Maybe her lifestyle got messed up."

"Like you can talk about lifestyles." Brandi knew too much about me. "Are you still screwing around with ..."

"We aren't talking about me."

"Fine." Shutting Brandi up was a win for me. "You know I like living vicariously through your stories, right?"

Brandi and I started in the RCMP at the same time. We were together every day for six months of training and talked almost every day since. While I had the steady course of my career, Brandi went on a different path. She took leave twice to have children. When I needed a family I joined hers. When she needed an escape I told her about my life.

"I have the training to do a facial reconstruction. I haven't done one in the field, but I could give it a go for Jane Doe, if you want. It would take a few weeks though."

"A few weeks? Let's try finding her ID the old fashioned way first." I had total faith that we would find her identity. She was a woman dressed well, no signs of drug abuse, clean body. Somebody was missing her.

Chapter 12

MY FIRST THOUGHT ON the Avery home was that it was a very polite looking house. It was a cottage not far outside of the city in a smaller hamlet. The front yard was ready for winter. The small trees were covered in burlap and tied with twine. The flower garden in front had been all dug up and the soil turned. It seemed familiar. The flower garden at my place had dead plants sagged over waiting to be covered by snow. I had no idea who planted them or when. Shit, they could have just been weeds for all I knew. A dog barked inside the home. A woman opened the door before we got up the steps.

"Mrs. Avery?" She nodded. "Corporal Faryn Steel and Constable Brandi Faye of the RCMP. I was hoping we could talk."

"Is it Jordann?" Her eyes were wide. She looked young to have a daughter in her twenties. She was tall, but the moment she spoke she slumped forward as if the stress of having a missing daughter was what was holding her up.

"May we come inside?"

"Sure. Ignore the mess." She swept a hand letting us enter before she shut the door. There was a baby stroller folded and standing in the corner by the door. A laundry basket was overflowing with tiny outfits. "Is this the part where you tell me I should sit down?" She stood there with her arms across her chest.

I decided she wasn't that type of lady. "Mrs. Avery, we have found a body that we cannot, as of yet, identify. We are asking relatives of people on missing person reports for DNA samples that we can compare to a sample from our Jane Doe. To be completely honest, I can't say one way or the other if this is Jordann."

"Why not show me a picture or get me to go make an ID?" She took in a quivering breath as she held back tears. There was music playing in the next room and the sound of a squeal.

This was the second time today that I had to answer this question. "There are complications with that. DNA is the only way we can get an identification. Constable Faye can tell you what we need in a minute. Can I talk to you a little about Jordann first?"

She led the way into the living room and sat on a grey flower pattern couch. There was a glass display case in the corner loaded with brass figures on lower shelves and crystal ones on the top. Some potted plants were by the window. A framed picture in one corner showed the lady and a young girl. In the other corner was a framed picture of a young woman graduating from high school. She had a yellow sash around her neck. Everything seemed to be covered in a thin film of dust. It reminded me of my grandmother's living room that was only used on holidays. The rest of the time you didn't go near it. This woman didn't flinch at our boots on the hardwood floor. The focal point of the room was the baby on a play matt on the floor. It's tiny hands tugged on the toys hanging from an arch.

"What can I tell you?"

I sat on the other end of the couch, barely on the cushion. Brandi squatted down to play with the baby's belly. "What does Jordann like to do? Does she party? Go dancing? Stay at home?"

Mrs. Avery pointed at the pictures. "She was an honors student. She would rather stay home studying than go out with friends on weekends. She played volleyball as a way to get ahead. She wanted to go away to college and then it all changed."

"What happened?"

"Her father died just over two years ago from an aneurism. It was sudden and unexpected. Jordann insisted on staying home and working to help out, so there went college. She said it was to help me cope, but I don't think she was coping with the loss herself.

She started working more, staying away from her extracurricular activities and that was when she started to go out. She was drinking. And she got pregnant. She was depressed before, but once Addison was born six months ago it got even worse. She wasn't going on social media or talking to me or to friends. A couple times she said everything was getting to her and she stayed away for over twenty-four hours without telling me where she was."

"Is that when she left?"

She shook her head. "She left me a note one day saying she was good and was going to stay with friends and for me not to worry about her. I thought it was going to be just for a little while, so I didn't report her missing for a few weeks. The officers said since she was a grown adult and there was no foul play expected there was not much they could do. They even suggested the note could be hinting at suicide. I don't think she would ever do that, but the more you think about it." Her voice trailed off. No parent wanted to think about that possibility, but that wasn't the worst thing that could happen to a child.

"Did you try finding her yourself?"

"Of course. I went to her work. They said she hadn't been there for longer than she had been gone from home. I called friends. I went to where she liked to go. I had her baby to take care of and my job, so I couldn't do it all myself."

"That's fine, Mrs. Avery. Does Jordann have a boyfriend? The babies father? Close friends she might go to?"

Her hands rubbed together. "Addison's father was out of the picture even before she was born. She had a boyfriend after that, but nothing serious. She seemed to stop talking about everyone the month or so before she left. They used to come over here a lot to hang out in the kitchen for snacks. That seemed to stop after she got pregnant." She wasn't tearing up, but she did look distraught about the whole thing. She lost her husband because of a freak aneurysm and then slowly lost her daughter. I really didn't want to be the one to tell her Jordann's face was half blown off.

"I'll need you to write the friends names down please." I passed over my notepad and pen "Does your daughter wear any jewelry?"

"I think she left most of it here. She was talking strange before I last saw her. A lot about cleansing. She took her heart necklace though. Her father gave it to her."

This was all filler. And a way to build who Jordann Avery was and if she was the victim. If she wasn't then this was a waste of time and everything usable was slipping away.

"Did she leave a brush or toothbrush here when she left?" Brandi asked.

"Her brush is in her room I think." She lead us down a hallway to a bedroom. There was a queen sized bed, made with hospital corners, an open closet with lots of clothes hanging, boxes on the bottom and stuffed animals looking from a shelf There was a dresser with a mirror on top where minimal makeup sat in the front with the hairbrush. "Take a look. I don't think she left any clues as to where she went. I've been through everything dozens of times."

Brandi pulled on blue gloves as she stepped toward the mirror and placed the hairbrush inside a plastic bag and filled out the label. We searched for a diary or journal in the usual hiding places with no luck. Her clothes were all neat and placed where they were supposed to be.

It wasn't that missing persons were not doing their job, it was that it was a hard job. If someone didn't want to be found then they weren't going to make it easy. Don't use bank or credit cards. Get off your cell phone and don't go on social media. In Jordann's case she had taken off before only to return a time later. There was no reason to believe there was any foul play involved. Human trafficking had come to Saskatoon, but this didn't feel like that. This was a young woman in a manic state who couldn't cope with her life at the time. If I had got this case I would have expected to find her body. Death by suicide. No body meant something else.

"Thank you for your time, Mrs. Avery." I had waited for Brandi to give me a nod that she had everything needed. "We should have DNA results with-in a few days. I'll let you know what they are either way." That was not going to be an enjoyable return visit. "One last thing, did Jordann ever mention anyone named Pony?"

Mrs. Avery shook her head. "She used to ride ponies out at Crooked Shoe Ranch."

We left her with a baby crying in the background and her mind all in turmoil. I wondered if she would want the body we'd found to be her daughter or if she would rather have her continue being missing.

Chapter 13

"YOU ARE JORDANN'S FRIEND?"

"Yeah, I guess. I haven't talked to her in, oh God I don't even know, months. She quit volleyball shortly after her dad died and we lost touch. I went and saw her when her baby girl was born but that's been it." Monica was listed as best friend on the list from Mrs. Avery. Obviously there was a lot about her daughter she didn't know.

"Why did she quit?" I dropped Brandi back at HQ leaving me alone to talk to Jordann Avery's friends. Officers had spoken to them when she was reported missing, so it was just rehashing what they had already asked.

She pushed her black hair off her shoulder. "I don't know. She just freaked out one day and said she couldn't stand being fake anymore. She couldn't take her dad dying I guess. She threw her duffle bag across the room and left. I tried texting her after but she never replied, so I stopped." Then I heard she was pregnant and then she posted on Facebook about her daughter. I went to see her. We had been best friends for years and I missed her. She just didn't want to see me."

"What was she like the last time you saw her?"

Monica's eyes rolled back as she searched. "Distant. She didn't say much."

The owner of Wilson's Deli was the next person I spoke to. "What was her attitude like?"

"Great, at first," Margaret Wilson, made me a sandwich as she answered my questions. "She had worked on weekends before her father died and was always happy. Greeted every customer with a smile. After her father's death Jordann was understandably upset, but she still came in ready to work and came in more often. It was okay for a while then she started missing shifts. I gave her some slack, but when she showed up drunk I had to let her go. That was six months ago."

"Was that the last time you saw her?"

"Ah, no. She came by after that asking for money. I said no and she got really mad and yelled at me."

"That was out of character?"

"Definitely. I never saw her get mad before."

She was the third person I had asked who said Jordann's personality had changed. She was going down a spiral and was the perfect customer for the Stable. "Did she ever mention a man named Pony?"

I got a no from her, so went and asked her former boyfriend the same question. Zack Brown stared at me for a moment. His lips scrunched up as he shook his head. "No. That a real name? She left me for a guy named Pony? Is that what you're saying?"

I ignored the question. "Did she give you a reason for leaving?"

"I was smothering her. That's what she said. I don't get how I was smothering her at all. I gave her her space, I didn't call or text a lot. I thought we had a good time when we went out. I never hurt her or anything. I treated her right. I was giving her money for the baby. I still give her mother money for Addison even though she isn't my daughter. I know what you're thinking. I wasn't the reason for her going crazy."

"That was the last time you saw her?"

"Yeah I think so. No, wait, I saw her a couple weeks ago working at the Farmer's Market. At least I think it was her." He adjusted his baseball cap letting some dandruff sprinkle down to his shoulder. He was polite looking. Short hair, clean clothes, clean fingernails...he looked like the kind of guy a mother would want a daughter to date.

He had an attitude, however, that made you question him. I had dated boys like Zack a long time ago. "I didn't talk to her or anything. I saw her talking to other people at the table. She didn't look the same. I yelled out her name and she looked at me, but ignored me completely, so fuck her."

"Did you recognize any of the people she was with?" This was all new. None of this was in the reports because it happened after. Maybe I should ask why he didn't report it.

He shook his head. "Never saw them before. There was girls and guys."

"What did the guys look like?"

"I don't know. Average. One guy had short hair, shaved almost. Another had long hair, like shoulder length I guess. I didn't get a good look and wasn't even sure if it was her. She looked right at me, but I don't know, maybe I was wrong. They had a sign on their table. Something about horses."

If someone saw the name Stable they might think it was about horses. If that was Jordann Avery two weeks ago then it could be her on the slab at the morgue. That would be connection number two to Pony. The car was stolen, but it wasn't reported, so was it really stolen or was that a story to cover himself after the car got stuck? Now this woman was possibly seen with them. Coincidence? Coincidences were not always what they seemed. It demanded at least another conversation with Pony.

Chapter 14

IT WAS ALREADY PAST 5pm, so most of the day shift was probably gone. I called Brandi anyway. "Feel like going for a drive? It'll take a couple hours."

"Official business?" I explained what I had found out and she asked if I had a warrant.

"There isn't enough evidence for one. I don't even know if Jane Doe is even her. I want to see Pony's expression when I ask. I need an extra body. Tell your hubby that I'll pay for him and the kids to have pizza."

"Fine. It'll give me a chance to grill you on your sex life. I'm still at the office, so pick me up there."

For a moment I thought about saying, forget it. I was riding the high of a new case. It was a rush and I didn't want it to stop. I knew others that hated new cases. I was morbid and liked the challenge.

Jordann was the same approximate age as our victim, same hair colour, same eye colour, she was already thought to be missing so that could be why no new missing reports were out there. It had to be her. Of course this could always be another rabbit hole just like the car was. But there was the connection to the Stable. She had to know Pony. He had access to the car. The more it rolled through my brain the more he was the perfect suspect. He got people to bare their souls then took advantage. Why would he kill one of his...clients?

"How many sex partners have you had?"

"Jesus, Brandi, don't beat around the bush." We had been on the road for most of an hour and she already got details on my latest excitement. I gave her what I wanted to. My life was my life and I really didn't like people knowing what was going on. Half the time I didn't know what was happening. "I don't have all their names in a purple notebook wrapped in two rubber bands on my bedside table, if that's what you want."

"That is rather specific isn't it?"

Chapter 15

NIGHT WAS FALLING AS we pulled into the Stable's driveway. The beetle and a pick-up were still there. As the car got close to the house motion sensor lights above the garage blared on lighting up the entire front of the house. More light streamed out from the windows and a tall pole in the back yard. The house was never quite in the dark.

"Officers," Pony stood in the open door as we stepped up, "what can I help you with now?" He sounded annoyed. Just inside the house was a small area with a washer and dryer, though this afternoon I had noticed laundry hanging from a line. A small set of stairs led up to a kitchen where a group were moving around and working together. I couldn't make out their conversations. A few looked down on us.

"Mr. Poniatowski," I watched his face cringe, "something came up and I need to ask you some questions."

He put his hand on the door and closed it slightly blocking my view of the others. His hair was a mess with strands down in front of one eye. I fought the urge to reach up and brush it away. How could he stand it there? "You don't have to agree with my chosen name, Corporal was it? But I don't have to respond to anything else."

I put my foot out to stop the door from closing. "I apologize." Before you ask, yes, that hurt. I heard Brandi make a noise behind me. "May I ask you my questions, Pony?"

He let the door relax open a little, however, his hand never left it. "You can ask, but I'm not sure how I can help you. I don't know who stole the car or where it went or anything."

"Have you ever heard the name Jordann Avery?" I stared at his eyes. I was hoping to see some blink of emotion. Was he happy for killing her? Did the sound of her name tickle his memory?

He stared right back. "Who is that person to you?"

"Someone I need to find." I took the picture out and showed him. "Have you ever seen her?"

A smirk crossed the man's lips. Where was that coming from? This time I fought the urge to smack it off his face. Over his shoulder he said, "River, can you come here." He turned back to me. "Is this like with Phoenix, Corporal? Can I call you Faryn? It's so much more informal." He pushed up his glasses and smiled.

"Please, do you know the woman?" I held up the picture again. He was playing a game that I didn't know the rules to.

"You called for me, Pony?" This was from a young woman that came down the set of stairs behind him. She had brown hair and a thin body. I recognized her instantly. Earlier that day I had seen pictures of her all around her mother's house and even a baby version. Jordann Avery.

Pony's smirk spread to a pompous smile. "River, these police officers are looking for Jordann Avery. Do you know who she is?"

"I might have seen her this morning in the mirror." Her lips pressed together in a tight grin as she stared right at me.

My nails dug into my palms as the fingers curled into fists. "Okay, very funny." My gaze fell on her. "Jordann, your mother doesn't have a clue where you are. She's taking care of your daughter. Have you ever thought of that? Have you?" My volume raced up. I wanted to grab her arms and shake her. Shake that stupid grin off her face. I looked at Pony. "How many more of your followers have missing person reports and families that don't know if they are alive or dead?"

"Followers? I don't know what you think this is, Faryn. Everyone who is troubled has to let their other life disappear before they can reach a place of renewal. For many that includes walking away from everyone they knew and everything they were. People like River and Phoenix. A lot of times your friends, your family, people you know and see every day are the ones that lead you down the wrong path. They chose to walk away. Their families have obviously chosen not to accept that they are no longer the people they once were. Is there anything else? Would you like to join us for supper, Faryn? Your friend can come in to. Its spaghetti with chicken."

I looked back at Jordann. "That the way it is? Was your mother and your daughter the cause of your problems, Jordann?" This anger wasn't about Jane Doe anymore. It was about the young woman's mother and the pain she was going through.

"Again, Faryn, her name is now River."

I didn't like the way he said my name. It was too familiar. His tone, when he said it, was like he had something special on me. "I'm not talking to you right now."

"This is my property and River is my guest, so yes, you are talking to me." His eyes burned with an intensity that made me afraid. He blinked and it all changed.

"Are you sure you can't join us?" The tomatoes and veg in the sauce are from our garden. The chicken we butchered this afternoon, Coyote made the pasta and River here baked the bread herself. Something wrong Faryn?"

The smile grew on the woman beside him. In her eyes was anger, however.

Did I say my first name when we came out here before?

Something was wrong alright. We had nothing. We were nowhere. Time was being wasted looking for nothing and these people were laughing about it. They were laughing at me. They were laughing at Jane Doe. I wasn't laughing. I didn't find any of this funny and I wasn't going to accept any of it. Something had to be done. Jane Doe was someone. These people were taking who they were and just throwing it away like nothing mattered while this poor woman didn't have a choice. They were all delusional. Or maybe I was.

I had nothing to say. Pony had nothing to do with Jane. I let my fists open and fingers stretch down at my side. "Nothings wrong, Pony." We looked into each others' eyes for a long time. I could hear Brandi breathing behind my left side. I felt eyes looking down at us from the kitchen. My eyes flicked to Jordann's. She was still smiling. "You call your mother."

Brandi and I got in the SUV and headed back to the city. As I turned off the road my eyes flicked to the mirror. Did I see headlights pull out of the Stable driveway?

Chapter 16

AS I STEPPED OUT OF the Avery house and breathed in the night air it chilled my insides and woke me. I raised my face to the sky and felt the tiny hits of cold from the snow that had started falling while I was inside. It had been a long time since I stuck my tongue out to catch flakes, I must have been a teenager when I found out what was in snow, but I did it then for a moment. My jacket was open and the chill made my nipples hard. As soon as we got to HQ from the Stable I dropped Brandi off at her vehicle and got into my Dodge Ram to go tell Jordann Avery's mother that her daughter was indeed alive, however wanted nothing to do with her or her own child. At first she was relieved. Then the questions came about why she wouldn't come home and who she was with. In a couple of short sentences I gave this woman the best news of her life and then broke her heart. For a moment I wondered if my own mother felt the loss she did when I finally left. Probably not. She didn't care about me when I was with her. Do the psychotic ever think they are wrong?

Mrs. Avery broke down as the tears and emotion flowed out of her. I sat with her for over an hour bouncing the baby girl on my knee until the grandmother calmed down. At least she knew, I guess. She knew where her daughter was and that she was fine, but what good was that going to do? Her daughter, for whatever reason, wanted to stay away. I knew what that felt like. I had always wanted to stay away from my mother, though I always went back. My mother had treated me like I was stealing her time, being a burden, and yet I went back to see her and was continually reminded of why I left in the first place. Jordann didn't want to go back to a mother and a baby.

I pulled my ringing phone from my pocket. I didn't recognize the number. "Hello?"

"Faryn? Its Paige...can you come to the emergency room?" Her words were slurred. It was around 10pm and she sounded drunk. When I was her age I was probably the same way. Now, more than ten years later at this time of night I was usually getting ready for bed if not already asleep.

I shoved my free hand in my coat pocket and pulled it closer to me. "What are you doing in emergency?" I was officially off duty, so I had changed into the black heels I kept in my back seat. They clicked on the stone walkway.

My head turned toward another sound. An engine was running. There were no cars moving on the street. I couldn't see any headlights anywhere, yet somewhere down the street an engine was running.

"I did something stupid. Can you come?"

Most modern vehicles had more or less the same body shape. That was why the round small body of a car up the street from where I parked was out of place. Was that a beetle? It was in the dark, so I couldn't see the colour. Did Pony follow me? The whole way back to Saskatoon my eyes flicked to the rear-view. A pair of headlights followed us the whole way. As we got into city traffic I managed to lose them. Or was it all something in my imagination? Was the 12 gauge the only weapon that had been stolen? I suddenly wished for my pistol locked away at HQ. My body tensed.

Paige made a noise on the other end of the phone, so I reassured her that I would be there soon.

I opened the back door of the twin cab and propped my aluminum bat so that the handle was over the middle tray of the front seat before climbing behind the wheel. The bat usually sat beside my heels along with a baseball glove. I knew the law. Having a bat was a concealed weapon. Having a glove with that bat made it sports equipment. I turned the key to start the engine then cranked up the heat and turned down the radio volume. The street lights on this street left much in the shadows. Trees would not let the light through. The truck was too big to do a quick turn to drive by the car to see if it was a yellow Beetle. That little thing could turn in the street easy and be gone before my lights were on it. I stared at the mirror.

Its headlights turned on. I shut my eyes from the blast of light. My skin erupted in goosebumps. Was it a coincidence that they picked that moment to turn the lights on? Were they watching me? The car still didn't move. What were they doing? Who was it? My finger found the door lock button. The click made me jump.

I reminded myself to breathe. This was stupid. I was a cop and here I was afraid of headlights. Pony had no reason to follow me. I had no reason to follow him. I had no reason to be afraid.

The headlights moved from the curb toward me. My hands locked on the steering wheel. I thought about the bat. I could grab it if needed. Unless there was another rifle. I watched the lights in the side mirror. It was moving slowly toward me. It was coming. I pushed as far back into my seat as I could. This was it. If I saw a rifle sticking out of the side window I'd have one chance to avoid the shot.

The car drove past. It was a Volkswagen Beetle and was yellow. My truck sat so high that I couldn't see the driver in the shadows of the cab. I glanced at the license plate, but didn't recognize the numbers and letters. I'd check with what Paige wrote down in the morning. Was this the same car from the Stable? How many vintage yellow beetles could be in the city?

I exhaled and took a few deep breaths as the tail lights turned the corner and disappeared. One was white instead of red. There was still something in my chest. I was an idiot. What did I expect to happen? Pony was a health and addictions healer, not a psycho.

"Okay, Faryn, you fucking idiot, time to go." That tiny pep talk made me put the truck in gear.

Chapter 17

I FLASHED MY BADGE at the security guard as I walked into the emergency room. Paige sat next to a wall with her elbows on her knees. Her hair hung down blocking her eyes from seeing me. There were a dozen other people sitting on plastic chairs waiting for their turn to be seen. A television above the pop machines played the news channel with no volume.

I dropped to the chair beside her. As I glanced at her. There was a U shaped tattoo on the back of her neck. Her hands were on her lap, one wrapped in a tea towel with red stains. I could smell the alcohol wafting off her. She was dressed in tight jeans and a white blouse. Her heels were on the floor beside bare feet.

"What happened to you?"

She raised the wrapped hand with one finger pointing out. "Men. Man. One man."

"Let me see." I unwrapped her hand. A splash of crimson dropped onto her shoe. "You're bleeding." Her knuckles were bleeding over the rings she must have put on after work. The back of her hand had a gash across it.

"Nice shoes."

"Seriously?" I rewrapped her hand. "What the hell happened? Were you attacked?"

Paige sat up and leaned back. Mascara ran down her cheeks. "I don't need a man, you know. Men just, they just use you and you're left with what? What?"

"Did a man do this to you?"

She hugged herself. Her foot twitched and kicked the shoe with the blood on it. "What's wrong with me, Faryn?"

"Nothings wrong with you. Tell me what happened?"

Her blouse was stained with her own blood. The buttons were not in the right holes and you could tell she wasn't wearing a bra. "I'm stupid. I take people at their word and that's wrong. That's stupid."

"Tell me what happened and if I have to arrest you or someone else," I tried laughing to ease any tension. I looked around to make sure no one was listening. Every time someone came through the door I expected a good-looking guy with hair falling in front of his eyes. Stupid.

Paige opened her eyes wide. They were wet and glassy. "The internet is what happened. You talk to men online, but you never really know, you know. Even when you know them you don't know them. People hide things. It's not like with a suspect. You can't see their eyes, so you don't know."

I rested my head back on the wall. "So you were talking to someone online and, what, punched the computer? You're going to need stitches."

She twisted her body and pointed at the triage desk. "They said I have to wait. Don't even give professional courtesy." She raised her voice.

"How did you get here? Did you drive?"

"I'm fine."

"Do you know what happens to a cop that gets a DUI?" I bit my bottom lip to squelch my anger.

"I ran into Tim at the grocery store." After a cup of vending machine coffee, black, Paige was a little more herself. "We had known each other in high school, but hadn't spoken in years." Paige was one of those people that joined the RCMP with the intention of returning home and helping her community. At least that was what she said. I was one of those who joined to get the hell out of my home town and stay away. "He said hi to me and we exchanged numbers and we started texting. It was just friendly talk. He said he was married, so he wasn't fooling me there, but he also said they were having huge problems and talked about separation. His wife is like model hot. Long legs, thin, blonde, big boobs, perfect face, so I didn't get it."

"Good looks doesn't mean perfect life. And you are good looking." The two of us must have looked like quite a pair. Her with her wrapped up hand, smears of mascara and hair all in a mess and me in these clothes I had been in all day and my hair being kept in check by bulldog clips. Paige was pretty. She had a thin body with curves in the right places, perfect cheek bones. I was a little jealous. Her best feature were those big doe eyes full of expression.

"Not like her. Anyway, Tim and I chatted online for a while. Nothing really sexual, just about life and shit, until we ran out of stuff to talk about. The chat went farther than it should have. Sex stuff about what we liked and wanted and would do to each other." She really didn't care who was listening. "Tonight I was drinking and he said his wife was gone, so I ended up at his place. We drank some more and shit happened. It started with kissing. I don't know. It gets a little hazy, until he pushed me off his cock and yelled that his wife was on her way home. That I remember. We yelled at each other as we got dressed. He pushed me out the sliding back door and I punched the glass as he shut it. I must have broke it because that's where I got cut." She pulled a black thong from her pocket, laughed and shoved it back in. She leaned forward on her knees letting her brown hair drift to the side. "Shit, I'm a fucking joke."

"You did something stupid. Learn and move on."

"I fucked a married man. And I fucked up my hand," I tried to keep my eyes from locking on other people's gazes as she told her story. They were either watching us or watching a sports replays on the small flat screen. "How do I explain this at work? I can't tell my supervisor. They already judge me for being a woman."

I hated those long laments about how women had it tougher than men. It was that way long ago and many years in the future it would be that way onboard the Starship Enterprise. Even in our police force with women in high ranking positions it was still a fight. Raise your fists or get out of the way.

"You're going to call in sick tomorrow." I took a long breath. "You know the area where my victim was found. I'll request you work with me for a few days and let's hope you don't need a cast." I wasn't sure if that was the right thing to do. Everyone was human and made mistakes. Maybe mine was covering for her. Amongst all my other mistakes. "You have to get your shit together though if you want to have a long career." It really wasn't my intention to sound like a mother.

"And what? Be single with a single life? I like having men in my life. I like having fun." Paige stared at a poster that showed the effects marijuana had on all the parts of the body.

"I'm not saying don't have fun. I'm saying if you want to advance your career you can't be punching windows and sleeping with married men." A couple of people were now openly listening to us. If Paige knew my own secrets she would have been crying hypocrite.

Paige turned in her chair to look at me straight on. "When was the last time you got laid?"

I felt the peoples' eyes on me. They wanted to know the answer. "What?"

"You single, Faryn? I don't want a single life." It was as if she forgot her sex question the moment it escaped. "I want to pick up other peoples' laundry and have my place smelling like a man. I want to be laid." A teenaged boy that had been throwing up into a bucket sat up a little straighter. Paige continued, "what if I don't want the single life? Can't a female cop have a family and a career?"

I liked my life. I had take-out in my fridge and sometimes ate over the sink. I didn't have to explain anything to anyone. Certainly not to Master Millennial with the ice cream pail. I let out a breath. She was still drunk. She was emotional. Stay calm, Faryn. "Of course you can have the family and career. Look at Brandi in Ident. She has a husband and kids. All I'm saying is make better choices. You have to work hard and do your job."

We both went quiet. The teenager wretched again. I counted ceiling tiles. I had worked hard at my career. I went where they sent me, I picked positions to further myself. I was a good cop. I had awards for the things I had done. I did my time at my last post and now there I was a supervisor in Major Crimes. Yes, I stayed single and didn't have children or a family, but that wasn't what I had wanted. I had no reason to feel bad about that.

"How is the investigation going?"

By the time we stepped out of the hospital it was close to midnight. Free health care was not fast health care. "What investigation? You can't investigate until you have a victim and I have no idea who she is yet. I spent all day chasing the owner of the car and then a missing person that wasn't even missing. I went out to the Stable again. Damn waste of time." The thing TV cop shows never expressed was the time that passed. Everything went so fast. In real life nothing did. "My truck is over here."

"My car is," Paige pointed to one end of the parking lot then looked across to the other end, "it's somewhere."

"Yeah, you can pick it up tomorrow. Tonight you will sleep at my place."

Paige groaned, but followed me. "I can drive. I'm sober now."

"You're tired." I studied the parking lot looking for the curved angles of a Volkswagen.

"What's next in the investigation then?"

I didn't have an answer for that.

DAY TWO
MONDAY

Chapter 18

I HIT THE SNOOZE BUTTON the next morning for the first time in a long time. My usual morning routine was to get up right away, dress and run to my gym. As the weather got colder I contemplated taking the truck, but I wanted to run in the morning air as long as I could. I met my trainer Emery at 4:30am to work out before running back home, showering, getting dressed and heading to work. Monday morning I was too tired and knew I would have Paige to deal with, so I texted my trainer before trying to get back to sleep. The joke was on me.

Paige was gone by the time I got up.

I lived in a small two bedroom bungalow on a quiet street. Like she had said at the hospital, I lived a single life. There was one bedside table in my room and no room in the closet or dresser drawers for anyone else but me. Light from the hallway glinted off a metal ring in the ceiling. The master bedroom was at the end of a hallway with the bathroom and guest bedroom on either side. Paige wasn't in the other bedroom. The blankets were left a mess. The rest of the house was open concept. Kitchen and dining area took up the same space with a small high round table and backed stools around it. The table top was half covered with paperwork and photo albums. The living room had a couch, lounger, flat screen that I barely turned on and a large bay window which looked out at the fenced yard. What more could a single lady ask for?

There was no note from Paige. She was a big girl and could take care of herself and her own business.

"Good morning, Faryn." Déjà vu. I didn't even make it to my truck.

"Hey, Cheryl." The snow from last night hadn't stuck.

"Didn't go for a workout today?" Her dog yelped.

"Worked late." I didn't want to blow my neighbor, Cheryl, off to keep relations, but wasn't going to give long winded answers either.

Cheryl was a well kept housewife. Her hair was recently coiffed and her clothes new and stylish. She probably even had a new ring to add to all the ones on her fingers. "Did you hear about that poor woman found up north? You must have. I'm so glad we have a police officer living on our street."

I grinned, not sure how to respond. "I have to get going."

"Okay," she tugged the leash and her little dog trotted along. Over her shoulder she said, "I'll get Wendell to rake your leaves."

I waved as I climbed in the Dodge. Her son would rake and I would pay him out of guilt. Guilt that, yet again, my yard wasn't right for the neighborhood.

Chapter 19

"WHERE ARE WE WITH THIS?" Sgt. Bisson sat behind his desk as Erik and I stepped into his office.

Every morning of a major crime investigation a triangle meeting was held of the three main people involved. The team commander, files coordinator and investigator discussed what happened in the past twenty-four hours and how to best spend the next. I spent this one telling them how much of nothing we had.

"Ident did find a fingerprint on the stock of the gun. They ran it through the system overnight, but there was no match."

"All that means is they don't have a police record." The sergeant leaned back in his chair. "What's your feeling on this Pony?"

"Something's off. I don't know what that is yet though." I left the Volkswagen and my paranoia out of the story. "I was thinking, the way Jane was dressed, it was for a night out on the town. I'm going to go to bars and show them a picture of her dress and what description we have. That's all I've got."

Bisson nodded. "It'll be like searching in the dark. Start with rural bars. There's one on highway 20 in Crystal Springs near the end of 320." Highway 320, which wasn't much of a highway, was the one that ran past Domremy and was just a few kilometers from the crime scene. All the small towns have a bar. I will be doing a press release with some information later this morning."

"Hopefully someone reports her missing." Hoping for the worst day in someone's life to identify the woman was not the greatest feeling.

"Any word on the autopsy?"

"It's being done first thing this morning. We should have a preliminary this afternoon." The full blown pathology report including toxicology and everything we ever wanted to know about Jane Doe would not be handed to us for four to six months. If I waited for that long more and more cases would be dropped on top of hers until this woman was lost. I didn't want her to be forgotten. I had to find out who did this to her as fast as I could.

I sat in another triangle meeting before I could even get started. For this one I was the team commander. Charlie Delaney was the investigator and Walter Belanger the file coordinator. The case was a series of house invasions in the rural areas where three people had already been hurt.

"Is that everything then?" I asked after forty minutes of going over what we already knew.

"That's it for the case, for sure, but I have a question about something else." Charlie waited for me to nod. "Are you a model?"

"Excuse me?"

Charlie put his hands out. "What? I was searching for your country music friend and saw modeling pics. Like you said, I'm an investigator.

"Are you stalking me now?" I gathered my things and left the conference room.

"I'm not stalking you. I wanted to support your friend." Bullshit. Charlie kept pace with me back to my desk.

As soon as we were there I turned on him. My finger poked his chest. "You do understand I'm your supervisor, right? Yes, I modeled when I was younger and do it sometimes for a photographer friend. Stay the fuck out of my life before I report it."

"Calm down, Faryn. I was just asking a question. Not my fault if you're ashamed."

"Suck my cock, Charlie!" Other heads turned in our direction. I bit my bottom lip as I calmed myself. Charlie turned and strutted away before I could say anything else. I wanted to say that I wasn't ashamed of any of it. All of the pictures were tasteful and I was fully dressed, okay mostly dressed with things covered. I worked hard to have my body the way it was and I was proud of it.

I signed out the Pathfinder and drove out of Saskatoon on highway 5 then 41. Kenneth Kissler, the registered name for the 12 gauge shotgun, owned an acreage near Wakaw Lake off highway 41. The property was amongst a set of trees, so it looked different than the typical Saskatchewan fields.

"This is my gun cabinet. They smashed it all to hell." The tall gun cabinet was dented and beat up as if a sledge had been taken to the lock. The colour of it reminded me of jeeps from the old TV show M.A.S.H. "Took the 12 gauge and all its shells. Took the 22 and thirty-ought-eight. This is the first hunting season since I was ten that I haven't gone out. That's forty-eight years of tradition. Been waiting for months for you all to find them. I'm not getting rid of the cabinet until I know I need a new one."

"Was this all they took?"

Mr. Kissler scratched his rough grey beard. "I gave the list to the cop that came. They took a computer, tools, some hunting knives, even food. They even took my pair of dress shoes. I only have boots and one pair of dress shoes and they took those. They trashed the place too. Broke windows and threw things around. My fridge was left open and the food was spilled all over. Somebody pissed in my boots. Who the hell does that?"

"You live here alone?"

"Oh fer sure. Sandra passed almost five years now. My son lives in the city. My daughter lives out west in Middleton, B.C."

"Anyone know you live here alone?" His home was full of memories. It was built of logs on their sides and stained caramel. As he showed me around he told me the story of how the logs came from the north and his wife, kids and himself did the work of pealing them to get ready to build. There were pictures and mementos of his life all around the room. You could tell he now lived a lot of his life on the leather lounger. He was older, but still strong. His hands were those of a man that never stopped using them.

"Anyone who knows me. I gave the Constable a list, there."

"Did I see a for sale sign at the end of the driveway?"

"Yes. The son has his thing and my daughter has her family out west. I need to move closer to the city. Not be so alone." His hand caressed a hexagon shaped center support log with animals carved and burned onto the tan wood. "It's time I think."

"Do you mind if I get your fingerprints for a comparison?"

"Fer sure."

As I got back on the road Mr. Kissler's words continued in my brain. "They trashed the place. They broke in through this door." They. He always said they, never he or she. Either he or the responding constable thought it was a group. Gang related? Did the person or persons that broke into that house kill Jane as well? Did her killer buy, steal, borrow or take the shotgun from the thieves?

I started my patrol of bars and taverns with the Crystal Springs Motel. Many villages had the same thing. Six or eight rooms to rent, daily drink specials and some sort of food item to draw people in. In Crystal Springs case it was fresh pizza. Others offered a lot of deep fried items. A few had actual cooks making actual food.

Most of the people I talked to in the bars where I stopped said the same thing.

"I'm looking for someone who might have seen a woman in this dress," a picture of the dress had been in the file emailed over. I couldn't really show a picture of a face with visible bone and brain matter. "She would have been in here Saturday night."

"Are you serious?" Bartender.

"Were you working Saturday night?"

"I was, but I don't pay attention to what people are wearing when I work."

"She probably would have been new. Would have gotten chummy with someone." By the tenth bar I had a splitting headache.

"No. I would have noticed someone new."

"Saturday? David worked the bar Saturday night. He won't be back in until tomorrow night. The same servers work then too."

I had just left the Greek Brew Pub when I heard the press release for the first time.

"Local RCMP are seeking any information pertaining to a woman's body found twenty kilometers north of Wakaw. The woman was believed to be in her twenties, 5'4 with long brown hair. She was found wearing a brown dress. Anyone with information on her identification or may have seen her Saturday night is asked to call..." I wondered what we were going to get out of that. How do you find actual leads amongst all the fake ones?

DAY THREE
TUESDAY

Chapter 20

I WOKE TO MY ALARM at 4:30am, got dressed in grey leggings, a T shirt with Stranger Things on the front and a grey hoodie and ran to the gym. I glanced over my shoulder at every turn, side stepped and looked behind me between turns. Usually the headphones would go in, music on and I would run without looking back. Not this day. I hadn't seen the Volkswagen Beetle since Sunday night and had no reason to think Pony or anyone else was following me, but I had that feeling. Call it a cop "spidy sense," women's intuition, whatever, but I had a feeling like someone was watching me. They were behind me. Maybe it was from constantly having Cheryl watching my place when I was home. Reality said she watched the whole neighborhood, however my mind said she was watching me. By the time I got to the gym I was breathing heavy. My eyes did a last sweep of the parking lot before going inside.

"Cute bunny hug." Emery flashed a smile.

I growled. In Saskatchewan they called hoodies bunny hugs. Why? No seriously, somebody tell me. Was it to do with the pouch pocket because then it should be called a kangaroo hug.

"How's your case going?"

I unlocked my gym locker. "You know, not easy when you can't identify your victim."

Emery was dressed in pink leggings and a sports bra. Her body was something to envy. I worked out and was toned and for the most part firm, but she was a fitness model. Muscles were where they should be and not overly developed. Her stomach still showed a little stretch from having children to make her human and not some Instagram fantasy. Her breasts were store bought and fantastic. "You'll figure it out. Faryn always gets her man. I heard the request for witnesses on the radio this morning. Someone will call in."

"Probably get more nutters than actual tips."

"Maybe you'll get lucky. Grady won't forgive me if I don't ask. Would you like to meet for drinks tonight?"

"Maybe. I'll have to play it by ear."

"Sounds fair. Let's go break a sweat."

I managed to get home and leave for work without running into my neighbor.

Chapter 21

"THIS IS CONSTABLE PAIGE Garrett of the Wakaw detachment. She knows the area the body was found in, so I asked her to join us." She had met me outside the back door to HQ holding out a cup of coffee. It was as if we coordinated our outfits with both of us wearing black trousers and a blue blouse, mine dark. I continued after Sgt. Bisson welcomed Paige. "I visited bars in the area, small towns and then the east end of Saskatoon asking about a woman in a brown dress and got the same answer from just about everyone. Nobody remembers the dress. Nobody remembers the woman. I have some places to go back to and I haven't gone up to Prince Albert yet. I'd be surprised if I get anything with it.

"I'm going to talk to Chuck about the home invasion investigation. Kenneth Kissler owned the murder weapon until his place was broken into months ago and it wasn't that far from the scene. Wakaw detachment probably took care of it. If we're lucky there's a connection to the home invasions."

"Autopsy?" Bisson was a man of few words.

"Being started within the hour. I will talk to Dr. Child later today and get his prelim."

"Anything from the press release?"

"A few tips," Eric said. "I've forwarded them to Faryn."

"Paige and I will look into them."

"It's been forty-eight hours. We need something." That was Bisson's way of telling me to go get something.

"Do you know anything about that break in I mentioned?"

Paige shook her head as we moved to the small conference room. "Just the basic facts. We've had a couple break ins in the area though. Kids from the city most likely."

"There's the super star!" Charlie rose to his feet and clapped his hands in a grand fashion.

"What the fuck are you talking about?"

He wore a sinister clown grin. Very Pennywise. "I'm talking about your stature as a music video queen. I mean you're no Courtney Cox in a Springsteen video or, or what's her name?" He looked to Walter and Paige for help that didn't come. "Saoirse Ronan, however you say her name, in that, that Ed Sheeran video. What's that one?"

I hated repeating myself, but in this case had to. "What the fuck are you talking about?"

"Galway Girl! That's the song."

"Charlie!"

"You're in a music video," he sat back in a leather chair. "Don't tell me you don't know about it. It's not much of a video anyway. Just pictures of you."

"What are you talking about?"

"Pictures. Like you in a bathing suit, you sitting in an old truck, sitting on a chair in the woods. Any of this ringing a bell?"

I stared down at him. For some reason his moustache was pissing me off. It was mocking me. This time I wanted to tear it off. "I meant the video. What damn video?"

Charlie Delaney smiled under the brown furry caterpillar that also seemed to turn up at the ends. "Go on YouTube and search, Faryn Steel I Want You. Go ahead. I can wait." We stared at each other. I wanted to pull out my phone and type in the search to see what he was talking about. I wanted to, however couldn't let him see he was getting to me. "It's by your friend, Jimmy -"

"Enough, Charlie. I have my own cases to get to."

"I'm just breaking the ice."

I slid a chair out and dropped into it. "You're just being a dick. Any news on the break ins?"

His eyes rolled. "No. I'm hoping for them to try selling something, but nothing has turned up."

"Is the Kenneth Kissler place on your list of home invasions?"

Charlie looked at the list of home owners and victims even though he knew it by heart. "No. Who is he?"

"The former owner of the shotgun that killed my Jane Doe. Get in touch with Wakaw detachment and get the details. See if it matches up. Paige can tell you who to talk to." I rose to my feet and spun around hoping to have the last word as I walked out.

"Jimmy is coming here on tour," was yelled out behind me.

I got to my desk, uploaded YouTube and typed in my own name. Sure, I had Googled myself once or twice to see if anything I didn't know about myself was out there. This was a whole new thing. I clicked on what came up and instantly there was the sound of guitar strumming and a picture of my face. Even my name was on it. Right away I recognized the deep soulful voice. "Hey, why do you run from change now?" Run from change? I walked away from a relationship which wouldn't let me be myself. There was no running. The pictures that rolled through the small video were mostly my modelling. A couple were pictures he took. I couldn't decide if I should be creeped out, pissed off or flattered. Pissed off!

Ten minutes later I got a text from Brandi asking if I had seen the video. I was obviously not the first person Charlie told.

Chapter 22

"LET'S GO." I GATHERED my notebook from my desk.

Paige looked up at me from where she sat. "What?"

"I'm getting out of here. We can check the tips from the press release and some more bars." Jimmy sang from someone else's computer. "I can't be here anymore." I headed for the door without knowing if Paige was even following.

"How was your workout?"

"Good. Can you drive? I have to go over all this shit that I couldn't in there." I handed her the keys to the Pathfinder without getting an answer and snatched up my ringing phone. "Corporal Steel."

"Corporal, Dr. Child. Do you have a second?"

"Have you finished the autopsy?"

The doctor moaned across the phone before he continued, "not quite. I wanted to call you with what I do know. Estimated time of death is between 2am and 8am."

"You can't narrow that down?"

"Nothing is exact, Corporal. Due to the cold night it's hard to say an exact time. I can't give you the exact cause of death either. I don't want to say gunshot until I'm done. I can say she had multiple injuries. This poor woman did not have a good last night. Assuming the gunshot was the final end, it was a mercy shot. I'll continue and email the report. Of course, you know everything is backed up. I'll try pushing it to the top of the pile."

"Thank you, Doctor." I hung up and relayed what was said to Paige. Time. Time was not something we had.

We were gone and on the double lane highway heading north toward the city of Prince Albert before Paige said anything else. "What was all that back there? That Charlie guy is a dick."

"He's a good cop." I flipped through the printed pages of phone calls after the press release went out. Thirteen phone calls with thirteen different tips. There was always the chance that Jane Doe was bar hopping between two cities one hundred and forty-two kilometers apart from each other. "He just isn't ready to take me as his supervisor."

"Maybe you should put him in his place. He sure was disrespectful."

She was right. Disrespect could spread like a virus. Someone with a cold doesn't wash their hands and touches a door handle. The next four people that touched the same handle all catch the virus and spread it on to others. Soon everyone has it and Corporal Steel is a joke. Nip it in the bud or be left behind.

"And who is this Jimmy guy?"

"Old flame who needs to be put in his place. What about your man?"

Paige shook her head. "I haven't talked to him and don't really want to talk about it now. I hope you don't mind."

"I don't mind. We have a lot of work to do."

Chapter 23

ELEVEN HOURS LATER I had Paige drop me off at The Greek Brew Pub on her way home. It was a popular spot that brewed a half dozen different beers in large vats behind a glass wall at the back and had a chef that matched those beers to food. For a Tuesday night it was busy enough to have a buzz. As I walked in Emery waved at me from beside the glass wall.

"Hey guys."

"Faryn," Grady stood from the corner table and brushed his lips against my cheek. "We were beginning to worry."

Emery's lips smiled on the edge of a wine glass.

"Sorry. It's been a long day. I still have to talk to someone before I can join you actually. I'll be right back." The Greeks Brew Pub was busy enough to have a buzz, but not so busy I couldn't have a conversation. I walked to the side of the D shaped bar where nobody sat and waited for the bartender. I showed my identification and introduced myself. "Did you work Saturday night?"

"Sure did."

"What's your name?"

"Antony."

"Antony, do you remember seeing a woman in a brown dress like this?"

He placed his hand on the back of mine and leaned in close to see the picture on my cell phone. "Is that blood?" Antony had thick arms with his left one covered in tattoos. He had the pretty boy looks you wanted in a bartender. He probably brought in the cougars. No, I didn't miss the irony that I was the right age to be labeled a cougar. "Nah, don't remember. Unless she danced on the bar I probably wouldn't have noticed."

"Nice ink." His sleeve had pictures of Greek mythology from a three headed dog to Medusa to even columns. He rolled his arm so I could see more. On his forearm was a symbol that the pub used as its logo. It was on their sign and even the coasters. It looked like a fat horseshoe with feet. "What's this one? It's the bars logo right?"

"Oh yeah, its Orion the last letter in the Greek alphabet. Dad says it means the end of everything, so he used it for the pub and the beer we make so it's like this is the last pub you ever want to go to and the last beer you should ever drink."

Funny how it looked like a fat horseshoe. Have I seen that before?

"Hey, I can probably get the security company to send you the footage from Saturday night. Dad has the whole place wired."

I flashed a smile. I could add his footage to the pile of security videos I had to go over from almost every other bar I visited over two days. The ghost in the brown dress.

"Constable, oh, Corporal. Sorry, sorry." Pony leaned in beside me. Damn he smelled good. "You look great."

I didn't know the black slacks and blue blouse I had been wearing all day constituted as looking good. I glanced down see my bra was showing through the open buttons. "Are you following me, Pony?" My voice shook.

He leaned close to me, his shirt touching my arm. "Maybe I should ask you the same thing. I do come here often. Maybe you've looked into me."

"I thought the Stable was about getting rid of addictions."

"I'm not addicted to alcohol. I enjoy it. I am not drunk. I am tipsy. You should come out to the Stable sometime for a tour. You will see that we are trying to do the right thing. Have a good night."

"You said you come here often. Were you here Saturday night?"

He had taken a step away and now fell back until his back was against the bar. "Didn't we have this conversation already, Faryn?"

"I don't think so."

Pony took a step back from the bar. "Yes, we did. I told you I went for a drive with some of the others. That's all we did was drive."

"Mmm right." Of course I remembered, dipshit.

"There you go accusing me of something again. Don't the police need proof for that?"

"I'm not accusing you of anything."

Pony rapped the bar top with his knuckles and sort of swayed forward until his feet caught up and he was walking. I watched him go to the far corner of the room next to a column and copy of a Greek statue. A Roughrider hat covered his private parts.

I waved for Antony. As soon as he was done pouring a couple of drinks he came over.

"Can I get you something?"

"Maybe. Did you see that guy I was talking to? Do you know him?"

"Ponyboy, of course. Pony and his friends come in here all the time."

They were watching us. "was he here Saturday night?"

Antony looked down at the bar as he rewound his memory. He tapped a pencil against the edge. "Um yeah, I think so. Came in around ten, ten-thirty. I don't know when they left."

"I think I will be needing that security video."

Chapter 24

"EVERYTHING OKAY," EMERY asked as I returned to the table. She wore a black corset top with gold designs placed across it. The top pushed what she had out. It was paired with tight faded jeans. I felt very under dressed.

"Great. How was your day?" I don't listen to them. I can feel the gaze of Pony and the others from the Stable on me. I saw Jordann over there, the guy with the short hair and a few others. In fact I felt like everyone in the room was watching me. They wanted to see what I was doing and what my next move was.

"You sure you're okay, Faryn? You haven't listened to anything we've said." Grady had the strong confident shoulders of a successful businessman and a clean shaven face. He had never been married, choosing to concentrate on his career over relationships. Emery had been married once and it wasn't happy. He was looking to take care of someone and she wanted to be taken care of. The couple matched each other. I never matched anyone.

"Sorry, I have this case on my mind. That guy I was talking to is a suspect and I guess he's distracting me. Sorry."

Grady slammed his hand down. "Let's get out of here. You have things on your mind and can't relax. You sure can't relax here. Let's go."

"No, no, we don't have to." Yes please. I looked to the far corner. From where we were seated I could not see the people at Pony's table. He was standing, so I saw his scraggly hair and eyes glaring at me through glasses.

"Yes, we have to, Faryn." Emery squeezed my hand. "You're not comfortable. We can do this some other time."

"I had someone drop me off, so I need a ride." A hand graced my thigh and the nervous tingles were replaced with a different kind of goosebumps. "Do you guys want to come to my place for a drink?"

As we walked across the pub I glanced in the direction of the Stable members. Pony was not only standing and staring at me, his body seemed to turn with us. On duty with a gun on my hip I'd take it as a sign of aggression. A warning. Out of uniform I didn't know how to take it.

I looked over my shoulder before I got into Grady's car. Being a major crimes officer the thought of personal protection when off work was always there. I didn't want to live in fear and having a personal gun for protection would emphasise that. I looked behind us for headlights following. There were none.

As Emery stepped past me into my house I took in her perfume. It was floral. Something from the Orient. "Don't pay any attention to the mess."

"We have 2 kids. This isn't messy." Grady tried brushing the light snow from his shoulder, but did nothing more than melt it into the fabric.

I felt uneasy looking down the dark hallway. My hand grazed my hip where my pistol was when I was at work and felt nothing but my slacks. I fought the urge to grab a kitchen knife and go room by room checking in closets, behind doors and under the bed. Fear. Somebody was watching. At least that's what it felt like. I could still see Pony's eyes staring at me.

"May I?" Emery fingered through my scrapbooks. "You were in lots of sports. Soccer, football, cheerleading." Grady stood close behind her half looking over her shoulder and half caressing the side of her body.

"My mom...I didn't want to be home with her, so I got involved with everything I could outside of home. She liked not having me around as much as I didn't want to be there, so she kept writing cheques. The sports I liked I stuck with."

"Glasses, Faryn?" Grady held the bottle of wine we stopped for on the way.

"Corner cupboard."

Emery chirped. "All Valley Under 18 Karate Champion. Impressive. And all of these gymnastic awards. Gold medalist New Balance Invitational. There's more."

"You have a thing for cartoons?" Grady gave up on looking for wine glasses, they were in the far back, and pulled out three mugs. Each with a different character on it.

"Characters really. Some cartoons, some comics and anime. I just always seem to pick them up." I took a mug with G.I. Joe soldiers on it and sipped.

Emery flipped a few pages. My mother didn't care about my accomplishments as a kid, so I kept newspaper and school newsletter clippings and photographs. "This explains the flexibility."

"Oh?" Grady smiled at me. It wasn't hard to tell what was on his mind, especially with the bulge in his pants.

"Faryn, show him that scorpion pose. In yoga class she can do things the instructor can't even do. Cocky young bitch."

My rolled yoga mat was on the dining table chair, so I put it down and did the forearm stand scorpion. My forearms were flat on the ground as I kicked my legs up so I was doing a headstand with my body straight up in the air. Slowly I let my legs drop to my back arching it until I was curved like a scorpion tail.

"Well you could have some fun right there," Grady said. He helped me stand up as I corrected myself and tugged my clothes back into position. Again I looked down the hallway and at the window.

"Are you sure you're okay?"

I let out a sigh. "Yeah. I just need something to distract my brain."

Grady clasped his hand against the side of my face and pulled my mouth to his. He tasted of sweet wine. His tongue caressed mine.

"Hey," Emery snapped. "What do you think you're doing?"

"Distracting her," Grady smirked. He released my face and asked if it was working.

"A bit."

Having a relationship with a couple could be a tricky thing, but I found it so much easier than with just a man. I never tried a relationship with a woman. It wasn't my thing. I didn't have the stress of financials and in-laws and mortgages. I had the fun times. I had two friends. It wasn't all about sex either. There were plenty of times that we just talked and enjoyed each other. It was a different world.

Emery pushed him aside. "How about this?" She put a hand on either side of my face. Her palms were hot against my cheeks, rings cool on my skin. Her blues looked back into mine. This wasn't my first time, wasn't even my first with this couple. Her mouth pressed to mine and our tongues touched. She tasted of cherry and wine. As she started to pull away I pushed my mouth hungrily onto hers.

A hand squeezed my ass cheek. Emery's nails trailed down my arm. My skin erupted with gooseflesh. Lips moved away from mine and my eyes opened. I looked in the woman's blue eyes for a moment until we both smiled and her bubble-gum tongue reached out, flicking my upper lip. Her fingers caressed over my breasts.

"Mmm that feels good." My mind couldn't help going back to Pony.

"You like that, eh?"

Her husbands hands were lower. One on my backside and the other squeezing in the front. My panties were getting damp. The uncomfortable feeling was welcoming. My eyes closed as Emery's full lips met mine again. Her nimble fingers tugged at the buttons of my blouse. As soon as it opened the man's hot mouth was on my skin.

There was a flash. A second of bright light against my eyelid. What was that? Emotion inside me making things flash like in the movies? Joy? Lust? Happiness? Another flash. My eyes popped open. Emery's opened too. She smiled and traced my jaw to my neck with her tongue. That flash wasn't something in my brain.

What was it then?

I couldn't stop the moan from slipping out.

My blouse fell to the floor. Victoria's Secret crumbled on top of it. The man was down on his knees working at my belt. A woman's hands squeezed my breasts. Her teeth nipped my neck. A finger and thumb tugged a nipple. The sweet pain made things firework through my nerves. She closed her eyes as she took one breast in her mouth and my hand slipped to the back of her head getting her to take more in.

"Harder. Just like that." I squeezed my bottom lip between my teeth. With my eyes closed I saw Pony's hair, his eyes staring at me. He smelled of leather and musk. Jimmy didn't smell like that. No! I opened my eyes.

My slacks slipped. The panties were tugged down over my ass cheeks and a tongue went inside me. My mouth opened.

"Oh fuck."

The living room window lit up. The light came through the dark glass brightening the open area for a second then putting it back into the dim glow from the kitchen light. Red lights swirled in my eyes. There was no storm, so it wasn't lightning. That window opened to my fenced yard. Car lights didn't flash there. What flashed?

Cameras flashed. The way light worked someone could be right outside that window and I wouldn't see them. They could be taking photos of my deviant life and all I could do was stand there. My senses kicked in. The refrigerator hummed. The furnace was blowing. A tongue was inside my pussy as another massaged my nipple. Something wet was running down my thigh. I could hear my heart pounding. There was slurping and moaning from the others. My knees were ready to buckle.

Flash.

Chapter 25

THERE HAD BEEN AT LEAST a half dozen flashes before the three of us moved to the bedroom. When they left I wrapped myself in my bathrobe and went into my back yard with a flashlight in one hand and a chef knife in the other. Nothing was out of place. Wendell had raked the leaves and left them in a pile. The ground was now covered in a light snow so there were footprints outside my living room window. Someone had been there. It had been a camera that flashed. By the looks of all the prints they had been there for a while and even moved around. There were skid marks where they probably moved quick when I looked at the window. I put my foot beside the print. It was close to the same size as my shoe. Pony had bigger feet. Maybe it was a younger person. I thought about getting Brandi to check out the foot prints for evidence in the morning, but the temperature went back up over night and the snow and prints vanished. In the morning it was just wet grass. I could ask around the neighborhood later and see if anyone else noticed a peeping Tom or strange flashes. Maybe it was just a horny adolescent who didn't know how to handle his raging hormones. My kitchen and living room were all open. I had stood in there naked many times. Someone could have stood out there watching me, violating their own body. Guess I put on a show for the little perve.

Somebody had been out there watching. Who? I felt like someone followed me the other night, but did they? For a moment I stood still looking out as if I could look back a couple hours.

I locked all the doors and windows, plus closed the blinds tight so nobody could see through. My bedroom smelled of sex, cologne and perfume that wasn't mine. I put the knife under my pillow and was able to fall asleep, but noises kept me opening my eyes. Do you know that sleep when your brain is still active even though your body isn't? I finally gave in, got dressed, got a taxi to HQ and went right for the gym in the basement. A cool shower after a workout and I was almost awake.

That was when I got a text from Brandi, we had a DNA match.

DAY FOUR
WEDNESDAY

Chapter 26

"HOW CAN WE HAVE A MATCH of DNA without having a name?"

"The magic of science. Do you want a coffee? Paige? We have much better coffee than they have in Major Crimes."

"Ethiopian," Oliver Faucher chimed from his desk.

"Love some."

On the walls were nature pictures taken by Faucher on his hiking trips. Another had blown up pictures of fingerprints and then maps showing northern Saskatchewan. On Brandi's desk were pictures of her with movie and TV stars. She liked going to comic and entertainment conventions and got pictures with a lot of stars. Her and Aquaman was front and center. Almost as forward as the one of her kids.

"Excuse me." I caught each of their gaze. "Unsolved murder, remember?"

Brandi snickered as she poured coffee. As soon as she was finished she sipped from her own mug. "The DNA from the sperm found in your Jane Doe is a perfect match for the DNA collected from the bed of Marta St. John, if you remember that case."

"Who is that?" Paige looked from one of us to the other.

"A rape victim from almost a year and a half ago, I think. She was raped in her home outside the city. No suspects, no evidence, nothing," unfortunately typical for a lot of rape cases.

"Yes. It was Constable Delaney's case," Brandi said.

As supervisor I was privy to the case particulars and, unfortunately, I didn't forget much. Marta St. John had come home from work to discover an intruder in her house. She said she lived in the rural area to stay away from the crime in the city, however, that didn't work. All the men in her life were interviewed with no suspects. Her rural home was far enough from neighbors to not be seen without some effort. A hunting ground for a random rapist. No matter how good it was for him with nobody else around to see him this just wasn't the place you would typically find one of those parasites.

"Found something else though." Brandi took another sip before continuing. "I checked other databases and found another exact match. This time it was to a rape victim in the city. Also unsolved. Six months ago. Lead investigator was Greg Vista with city police."

Chapter 27

"ONE PULLED PORK SANDWICH." I dropped a rolled up brown paper bag on Greg Vista's desk, pulled a chair over from another and sat in front. For this one I went alone leaving Paige to watch security videos from all the bars we had visited. To be honest it was busy work. "You asked me to pick something from the Samich truck, so here you go."

"Thank you. I've been too busy to go get something." He extracted the panini sandwich and gave it a cursory inspection. "No coleslaw, right?"

"Yes there's coleslaw! Fuck you. You can't have a pulled pork sandwich without the coleslaw and their apple slaw is amazing. It's just not right if you do that."

"Since when are you a foodie, Steel?"

"Oh man. The guys on the Samich Food Truck do it right. A good pulled pork is dry rubbed and then slow cooked for hours. They pull it, add homemade sauce to it and put it on a freshly baked bun with coleslaw of apples, cabbage and..."

"Ew, there's cabbage?"

"How can someone so big be such a pussy when it comes to food?"

This wasn't the first time I had to deal with Sergeant Vista of the Saskatoon police. He was solid. Both in features and personality. His square jaw covered in trimmed dark whiskers looked like it could take a bowling ball and never flinch. His broad shoulders were muscle. On the investigation side of things he had a good record of getting his man. As far as I knew, and was told, he was a good cop. "Can we talk about Naomi Fuller."

"Right, I pulled the file after you called. Six months ago Naomi Fuller was at the Greek Brew Pub. She had more drinks than she should have and decided to walk across the park that's right by there to get to where she lives. She was attacked. She got hit on the side of the head and pushed into the woods in the south corner. That's where she was raped."

"You're a fountain of information. You said the Greek."

"Yes, have you been there? They make a great lager."

"I was there last night, actually." Pony.

He took a bite from his sandwich and only chewed half before talking. "You're going to go talk to Naomi anyway, so she can give you the gritty details. And are you going to tell me anything about why you're interested?"

"We might be working the same case, Greg. Any suspects?"

"There were a couple rapes in the area over the prior months," he still hadn't finished chewing, "but no suspect for those either." Swallow. "Sent the sperm in for DNA, but that came back with nothing. Talked to all the men in her life. She swears nobody she knows would have done it. She didn't really want to pursue it. She has a reputation as a party girl, so..." Greg shrugged his shoulders.

"Don't even go there, asshole. Nobody asks to be raped and there is no justification in the world for it." I looked around, realizing I had suddenly gotten very loud.

"Calm down. That's not what I meant."

"What did you mean then?" I knew he wasn't the type to be an asshole male about what was and was not rape.

"We checked everyone she knew. We watched surveillance video of the bar and contacted everyone we could. My theory was, and still is, that someone saw her stumble out of the bar. She admits she was three sheets to the wind and she had drugs in her system. They followed her into the park and took their chance. She posts pictures of herself in her underwear on Instagram and Snapchat and who knows what else. She has a lot of followers on those sites and tags where she goes. Maybe it was a fan. I don't even know if that had anything to do with it." He had put his sandwich down. "Oh, her shoes were taken. Probably to stop her from getting help quickly. The ground is pretty rocky there. We never recovered the shoes. We still have the surveillance video, so you are welcome to take a look."

"Thanks. I have some possible suspects that I can look for."

"I'll get it on a memory stick. Are you going to share the suspects name?"

"Not yet. And what do you mean the DNA came back with nothing? My DNA came back with a match to your case and one from a year and a half ago."

"They said there was nothing. Maybe they didn't check the national database. Not the first time they have messed things up."

Chapter 28

"MISS FULLER, I KNOW this is hard, but would you mind going over the assault with me?"

She scoffed. "What would you know about how hard it is? Have you ever been raped?"

"Not physically, no." We sat around her small dining table in her small apartment. It was much more of a single persons' place than mine was. "My mother would tear me down. She'd tell me I was a loser and would never accomplish anything. I know it's nothing like physical rape. It affected me for a long time. Still does. I'm sure your attack affects you in ways I can't imagine."

Her eyes rolled and lips pursed. "You had it easy. I did to. I was lucky," it was such a whisper that I almost didn't hear it. "I was so drunk I think I passed out because I don't remember much." From the look on her face she remembered a lot more than she thought she did.

"Did you go to the Greek with anyone? Friends maybe?"

"I went alone. There were some people there I knew and I sat with them, but I didn't go to meet them or anything like that." Naomi was a brunette and had that pretty girl next door thing going for her with a bit of an edge from the piercing in her cheek. Her eyes, however, had a darkness to them. I bet they didn't sparkle when she smiled. I wondered if that had been there before the rape. "Stupid, right? Going to a bar to meet strange men. You probably think I sound desperate."

"I'm not here to judge you and I go out alone plenty. Was anyone watching you at the bar? Maybe they were giving you attention you didn't want?"

"Maybe, I don't know. I got really drunk that night. I wasn't looking around at anyone, so maybe there was someone. I never got that behind feeling, you know? That feeling that someone was behind me, like, watching me. I didn't get that. I get it, like all the time now."

"You go to the Greek often?"

"Once or twice a week. Saturdays for sure. I did anyway."

"Did you always walk through the park and take the same path?" If she followed the same pattern every time she went drinking then someone who knew that could have been waiting. It could have had nothing to do with the bar at all.

"Yes."

"Have you ever seen anyone along your path? Anyone watching you?"

She shook her head.

"And you never saw whoever attacked you?"

"I remember hearing something behind me, but before I could turn there was an arm around my neck and I got hit on the side of my head." A couple fingers went to her right temple in memory. "I don't remember hitting the ground or being dragged deeper into the trees, but the police told me that's what happened." Her arms started trembling. "I don't really remember anything else. I'm told I'm lucky." She took a jagged breath.

"How did you get the scars on your throat?"

There were several healed scars of various sizes across the front of her neck. Little white marks that most may not notice. She gingerly touched them with her fingertips. "The detective said he must have held a knife to my throat as he ... I don't remember anything until I tried getting up. I couldn't find my shoes and my feet hurt as I walked home. When I got there my neighbor saw me and called the police. That's all I know."

From Vista's report the rapist likely used foreign objects to violently rape her. There was bruising and tearing to both her vagina and anus. It was a good thing she didn't remember, if that was true. Even if her brain didn't her body did.

"What kind of shoes were they?"

"I don't know. Black heels. I wore a short block heel so walking through the park on the path wouldn't be that bad. I bought them years ago at Walmart or something, so they weren't worth anything."

"Naomi, is the name Pony familiar to you?"

Her brown eyes were swollen with tears as she looked at me. She quickly wiped them away. "Yeah I know Pony. He was at the Greek that night."

"He was?" I had him. He had been there. He was our rapist and our killer. "How do you know him?"

Naomi lifted her shoulders. "I've known him for a while. I first met him at the pub and we hung out sometimes. Why are you asking about, Pony?" She wiped her cheek again though no more tears had fallen.

"There was a DNA match from the sperm from your rape kit to sperm found on a recent victim from this weekend. Pony is a suspect. Is it possible that he was the one who raped you.?"

"No," she said instantly.

"How can you be so sure? You said you didn't see your attacker."

"He didn't have to rape me. We had sex. In the bathroom at the bar that night." She stared at me as I stared back. What the hell was this? "If it's his DNA that's how it got there."

"What? Sgt. Vista didn't say anything about this." I recognized the panic in my voice. Everything I thought was falling apart. Again.

Naomi crossed her arms. She didn't want to be doing this and wouldn't hold my gaze. "I didn't tell him. I knew they were already thinking I was a drunk slut anyway, so why would I bother? I heard the nurse talking to him before he even saw me. They thought I was just some bar skank."

"You had sex with Pony in the bar bathroom?" I didn't think it possible, but that was one thing I had not done.

"Yes. What don't you understand? I had fooled around with Pony before and I had a bad day that day, so when he suggested it I went for it. We screwed in a stall and no, I don't remember if he wore protection. It was a sudden in the moment thing, so probably not."

Chapter 29

MARTA ST. JOHN INVITED me into her two story home. "Is there something new with my case?"

I stepped inside after wiping my feet on the mat outside. "Possibly. How have you been?"

Her shoulders bounced. Her dark brown hair was tied in a bun at the top of her head. She looked a lot like the woman I had already spoke to. "Surviving. I finally started talking to someone about what happened and that helps." She stared off into space and I just let her. After a moment she blinked and looked at me. "I haven't heard from Corporal Delaney in a while."

"I apologize for that. Something has come up and I have a few questions to ask if that's okay? Like, have you ever been to the Greek Brew Pub?"

"Not since I quit working there. Do you want coffee?"

"No, thank you. You used to work there?" Charlie had checked into her history and the Greek was not mentioned in any report.

She made herself a mug with four spoons of sugar. "Up until a few months before...before what happened. I told Constable Delaney about it. Nothing bad ever happened there I couldn't think of anyone looking at me funny or giving me too much attention or whatever."

"You told Constable Delaney about working there?"

"Yes."

And he didn't at least write it down? Fuck!

"Did you happen to meet someone named Pony when you worked there?" I could work around Naomi and Pony having sex before she got raped. It didn't mean he was innocent, but gave doubt. Maybe he got off on violating women who knew him. He would not be the first.

"No, I didn't."

There went that idea. There was still a chance that the Greek was his hunting ground. He had Naomi there. He could have met Jane Doe there and maybe she didn't want to go to the bathroom stall. He might have seen Marta when she worked there and got obsessed with her. Her rape took place here, out of the city, so how did he find her address? It was a year and a half ago, was he a patron at the Greek then?

"I met him at the Stable, not the pub," Marta said. "I realized after I met him there that he had been in the pub, but I never talked to him there."

The air left my lungs. "What? You went to the Stable?"

She nodded. "I broke up with this guy I had been seeing for years, Antony, and I wasn't doing good with it."

"Antony the bartend at the Greek?"

"And son of the owner. We dated for over three years. Even talked about marriage. I couldn't handle going to work and seeing him every day. I would get so stressed out and crying every night. I couldn't stay there." She rubbed an eye. "Pony was a regular at the pub, but I never spoke to him other than taking orders and delivering food. I didn't even know who he was until I went to the Stable." She swept away hairs that had fallen in her face. "I had heard about it and thought I'd give it a try. It was that or doing something stupid to myself. Pony helped me realize I was in a better place without my ex. I must have gone there a dozen times over a couple months and then Pony and I started something."

I was lost. This was all outrageous to me. He was there the whole time. He was in her life and doing his thing.

"It wasn't that serious, so I wasn't upset when we stopped. And then," her gaze fell, "You know what happened. I thought about going back and talking to Pony after, but it wouldn't have been appropriate with our relationship."

"Did he help you the first time?" In my head I was looking for the fraud that was Pony. He was looking for the vulnerable and a way to exploit them. I'll heal you then fuck you.

"Totally. I wished I could have gone there after the attack. Why are you asking about Pony?"

"DNA evidence. Pony is a person of interest in another case and his DNA came up as the unknown in your case. How well do you know him?" My mouth was dry. Maybe I should have taken that coffee.

"He didn't rape me, if that's what you're going for. He didn't have to."

"You're sure?" The report said Marta had been aware during her rape. The man had worn a knitted mask just like Stranger Danger, tied her wrists to the bedposts and did his thing.

"The man had different eyes. He wore a mask, but I could still see them. Blue, piercing eyes. Pony's are distinctive. Pony had been here the day before and we made love. It was an impulsive and stupid thing that neither of us expected, but nice. He was always nice. If it's his DNA that's how it was found. He didn't tie me up. He didn't rape me and sit on the bed after like he was catching his breath. It wasn't Pony. He was only ever good to me."

"I'm lost, Marta." I could feel a headache coming on. "Did you tell Constable Delaney about this?"

"I don't remember. I might not have. Pony had been in jail before and knew the police would go after him and not bother with looking for the rapist."

Seriously? No, not suspicious at all. This was no different than those women that get beat by their man but are so blinded by love or what they think is love that they don't do anything. Of course, I had been one of those women. "Okay then. Is there anything else that you have recalled since it happened?"

"Um, a pair of my good heels went missing. I realized it a week later but I might have just misplaced them. I don't know if it was that guy or what, but I baby my shoes. You can look in my closet and see that every pair has their own spot and they are all covered. I have tubs in my garage for different season shoes. After I wear a pair they are cleaned and put back in their proper spot. I went to get one of my favorite pairs, um these strappy opened toe black ones with a spike heel, the week after and there was nothing there. I searched all over for them and then realized the last time I had them was that day. Of course I had a breakdown." Marta had to finish her coffee before she could continue. "I wore them out and then placed them on the chair in my bedroom before he walked into the room. He had the knife in his hand, the mask on and said my name...after that I forgot about the shoes."

Chapter 30

"FARYN," PAIGE JUMPED up from behind my desk.

I said, "in a minute," as I marched past her. "Charlie? Where's Constable Delaney?"

"I'm here. What?" He came out from the coffee room. Brown liquid spilled over his mug onto the floor. "Shit."

I jumped at him. "What kind of bullshit job did you do on the Marta St. John rape case?" My anger had built during the drive back to the city.

"Who?"

"Marta St. John. Raped in her home a year and a half ago." I forced the files of the two victims against his chest almost pushing him back.

He put his mug down on the closest desk, after spilling a little more, and took the flipped papers. "Okay, let me think." He barely glanced at it. "Yeah, there were no suspects, not much evidence. It's been at a standstill."

"Why didn't you take note that she worked at the Greek Brew Pub months before the rape?"

"It wasn't relevant." He held the file out. I didn't take it so he put it on the desk and picked his mug up.

"Wasn't relevant? How about that she knew this Pony guy or that she had been going to the Stable? His name would have been flagged in the system. Instead I have to deal with incompetence! Two cases where this guy could have been caught and the investigators didn't do their fucking jobs."

"Two? What other case?"

"City police, so it wasn't you." Truth be told I was just as mad with Naomi Fuller and Marta St. John. Victims, eye witnesses, investigators...it all came down to dealing with the unpredictable human element. Any one of them makes a decision on what should be told and reported and the whole machine could implode. Charlie stared at me with his mouth wide, so I continued. "DNA from Marta St. John's sheets matched DNA from a rape in the city. Pony had sex with both women and in in both cases the women never told the investigator," I knew what he was going to say so I raised a hand to shut him, "and these great detectives didn't do their jobs. It's the same DNA that was on Jane Doe. The first two women knew Pony. His name wasn't even in your file, Charlie. The Greek isn't even in the file. The first two victims have a connection to Pony and the pub. The bartender says Pony might have been there Saturday night. He isn't sure. He. Is. My. Guy. If any of this was noted I could have made the damn connection sooner. Or better yet, he would be in jail and this poor woman would be alive."

"Pony was at the pub Saturday."

I turned to Paige. She nervously pulled at threads hanging from her bandaged hand. "What?"

"He was definitely there. He's on the security footage. I think we can get a picture of Jane Doe too."

"Show me!"

Paige took my chair and brought up a video onto my computer screen. "The video was dropped off while you were gone." The scene showed the bar I had been in the night before. It was a lot busier on the video. People circled the bar, every table was taken. It was not the kind of place where people danced. A lot on the silent video were milling around talking. You could almost hear the buzz of dozens of conversations. The bartender I spoke to was behind the bar along with another. I could see how they were too busy to notice one woman.

"See here in the corner? Isn't that Pony?"

It was the same corner he had been in when I had been at the pub. There was his shaggy hair and the way he stood out from the other Stable members. "Yes, that's him. Have you seen the Jane Doe on here?"

"I haven't looked for her yet. Not totally. I saw Pony and wanted to tell you."

"You bitch!" Charlie reached around me and threw the Marta St. John file onto my desk. I had forgotten he was still there.

"Excuse me?" At first I wasn't certain he was talking to me. I heard everyone's heads turn as they watched what was going on.

"You bitch about me missing shit. Did you even read these files?"

"Of course I did. I spent the whole day interviewing the victims." Our voices rose. I glanced at Bisson's door.

"Then you know that Marta St. John's rape was completely different." Charlie stared at me. "Naomi Fuller was raped and sodomized with a foreign object. So was your Jane Doe. Marta St. John was tied to a bed and physically raped. Not the same guy."

"The same DNA was at all the scenes. Pony had relations with the first two women and I believe we will find the third woman on this tape. Don't you even dare accuse me of doing a bad job."

"Maybe you're too distracted by showing your ass in music videos."

My fingers curled into fists. "You're pushing your fucking luck, Chuck. As your supervisor I'm telling you, you did a piss poor job. It cost me a -"

"Fuck you with your supervisor shit. That's fucking bullshit."

"Delaney! Steel! In my office." Bisson's voice boomed over everything.

Chapter 31

"I HEAR YOU'RE HAVING a shit day." Brandi handed me a Tim Hortons coffee after I opened the front door.

"Bad enough that I needed something stronger." I held up the tumbler with shiny brown liquid and ice cubes inside.

"I heard Bisson chewed your ass off?"

"You hear a lot. He said we were both lucky to not be suspended. He made us both apologize."

"That hurt?"

"Yes. You coming in?"

"Are you going to call me incompetent?"

"Are you going to intentionally leave shit off a report?"

Brandi's shoulders shrugged. She still wore the tactical blue uniform from work, so I didn't bother asking her in for a drink. "It happens, all the time. People leave things off reports because they don't think its important."

"Well this time it might have cost a woman her life." Maybe if Charlie had dug deeper or Naomi and Marta had revealed more, Pony could have been stopped and a woman not killed. Guess I had my primary suspect. "What are you doing tonight?"

"Good change of subject. The Man is taking me out tonight." Brandi's husband did most of the parenting of their children. He wrote mystery and thriller novels, so staying home gave him the opportunity to do that. In arguments, and I'm a witness, he referred to himself as The Man. Brandi called him that as an inside joke. "He wants to go see this country singer he might have heard of from a YouTube video I showed him. A guy named Jimmy from the west coast."

"Are you fucking kidding me?" Jimmy was in town. The camera flashes last night. Stalker.

"I can convince The Man not to go."

"No, you go. You can tell me all about it tomorrow."

"And you can tell me all about your apology to Delaney."

"Forced apology," I emphasized. "My fingers were crossed."

Chapter 32

JIMMY.

My eyes opened. It was that moment when you wake and don't know where you are for a second.

I had gone to bed with a bowl of hummus and a bag of baby carrots. They were on my bedside table next to the glass of wine I had switched to, but barely touched. The latest Kate Kulig novel was beside my pillow. The murder mystery novel somehow took me away from the investigation and relaxed me. I only made it through a couple pages before drifting off. Didn't even get to turn the lights off.

Jimmy appeared in my dream. He was playing guitar on a stage and taking pictures of me. I don't know how he was doing it with just two hands. He was staring at me with that judgemental way of his.

Knock, knock, knock.

I looked at the open bedroom door. The banging had been beyond that. Far away almost. Someone knocking. Was that what woke me?

Knock, knock.

It was the front door. Something wrong with Brandi? A neighbor needing help? It was never anything good.

My bare feet padded on the hallway floor. The light over the stove was still on. I glanced at the living room window. Everything was black beyond it. There was a rush in my chest.

Bang, bang!

I stopped moving. It was dark beyond the front door. What happened to the motion sensor light? I flipped a switch. Light flared outside. I looked out the window beside the door. There was nobody there. Did they leave? Somebody had been knocking on my door. It wasn't a dream.

I unlocked the door and opened it quickly. The spring in the glass outside door make a pop and hiss as if it finished closing. There was nobody there. There were no vehicles on the street in front of my house or in the driveway beside my truck. Something caught in my throat. What was this?

My gaze dropped to what was on the wood slats of the front deck. I looked all around again then opened the outside door. It creaked.

I slipped down to a crouch, my eyes scanning all directions as I did. There were four 4x6 photographs. The glossy prints felt hot in my fingers. The top one was of Emery with her tongue tickling my nipple. Another showed me with Grady in my mouth.

Caught.

I looked up. Left. Right. Who left these here? They knocked on my door at one in the morning and dropped these for me to find. Jimmy was in town. He didn't like my lifestyle and had harsh words for me before. Would he escalate to this? Would he torment me?

Bang, bang, bang, bang.

"Fuck!" I jumped back inside and slammed the inside door. My fingers found the deadbolt. The pictures slipped to the floor.

The bangs had the echo of glass being hit. The living room window. What the hell was going on?

I made it to the window in long strides and turned the yard light on. Everything out there lit up. The area where the camera man had stood, the yard. Nobody was there.

Bang, bang.

Bedroom window.

Bang, bang, bang!

Front door.

Bang, bang, bang, bang!

Bathroom window.

It was more than one person. My heart pounded. What the hell were they doing? I ran to the bedroom. They had the house surrounded. What did they want? Who were they?

Something banged the window. I screamed. Fuck. I grabbed my phone.

"This is Corporal Steel. I need a car at my residence." Another bang on the window. I held my breath. "Someone is outside banging on the doors and windows." I gave them my address as I tried to control my voice.

Bang! Bang!

Bang!

"I called the cops you assholes!"

Bang! Bang! Bang!

"I am a cop!"

Bang! Bang! Bang! Bang! Bang!

Silence.

I began counting the seconds. How many were out there? Where were they? Did they go? I looked down the hallway. The quiet itself was frightening. Did I lock the front door? Yes. There were no sounds, but what were normally there. The furnace, the fridge humming, grandfather clock in the living room ticking. There was nothing outside making noise. Maybe they were just waiting for me to open another door.

So much for getting more sleep.

DAY FIVE
THURSDAY

Chapter 33

"DO YOU WANT TO FILL me in on what happened last night?" Sgt. Bisson stared at me with his fingers interlocked on the top of the table. We hadn't even started the Triangle Meeting yet.

I shook my head. "Some neighborhood punks on something were knocking on my windows and doors trying to freak me out. I thought it best to call it in and frighten them away. They were gone before the car came."

"Did you get a look at them?"

"No, afraid not." I should have said something about the tape over my front motion sensor light or the camera flashes the night before. This wasn't something for work to worry about. They were my problems. As soon as I had a chance I would talk to the people I lived near and get to the bottom of it. "It's nothing Sergeant. City cops are looking into it."

"Then let's get started on the Jane Doe case. Is there anything new?" He looked at Saunders and myself. He wanted us to announce something grand. He wanted us to have the killer.

"You heard everything about the rapes and DNA yesterday," I said. "I'm going to see about any cases where people are missing shoes." I saw the boss's eyebrow rise in disbelief. "We have Pony on the security video from the Greek Brew Pub on Saturday night. He went in with who we believe are other members from Stable. They sat in a corner and were there a few hours. Jane Doe came in and sat near them with some others. Over an hour later she was in the corner where Pony was. She left and he left a few minutes later and was then followed by his people."

"Do we have enough to bring Pony in?"

My head swayed side to side. "It's all circumstantial regarding the rapes and less than that with the Jane case. We think we have her picture on the security video at the Greek Brew Pub, but not sure."

Constable Saunders slid the best picture the computer geeks could pull from the video of a brunette woman in a brown dress. It showed ¾ of her face, the parts that were missing when we found her, but it was more than we had before.

"We can release this to the press. We might get lucky." Bisson looked at me as if waiting for me to say something.

"I have a plan," I blurted out. "Pony invited me to tour the Stable. I'm going to go out there today and get him to show me around, introduce me to people. I'll get a sense of him, talk to some of the people that go there, see if I can find anything out, see if I can pick out who else was at the pub Saturday."

"You won't have a warrant."

"Don't need one if he invites me in. If I see anything I will call it in and sit on it. Constable Garrett will come with me and I'll have Wakaw detachment on alert. Everything will be fine." Famous last words.

Bisson leaned back in the chair. "Famous last words. You're walking a fine line, Corporal Steel. Bring me back a killer."

Chapter 34

I CLIMBED IN THE PASSENGER side of the Pathfinder and had my phone to my ear before Paige had us out of the city. "Vista, its Faryn. Any chance you can do me a favor?"

"Another one? You gonna try solving another one of my cases?"

"Not this time. I need to know if there have been any disturbances in the Lionshead area. Peeping Tom's, people banging on windows and doors at night, anything like that. I'll get you a pumpkin pie blizzard.

"No pie pieces?" I could hear him scribbling notes. "This for a case?"

"No, it's personal. Someone's been messing around with me."

"I'll ask around and get back to you."

I hung up the phone and saw Paige giving me glances. "Some trouble in the hood? Did your mom get scared?"

"Yeah, she's sending me to live with my aunty and uncle in Bel Air."

She smiled and her eyebrow arched.

I unfolded a brochure on the Stable. I had already gone over it a dozen times.

"What do you think you would go there for help for? What are you addicted to?" Paige was one of those people that got bored in a vehicle. She had to talk.

I shook my head. "Nothing. Don't smoke or do drugs, just drink casual. Pretty boring."

"There's nothing you're addicted to?" Paige looked at me with that eyebrow up.

"I don't think so."

She hummed and I went back to the brochure. I was nothing like River or Phoenix. I wasn't lost in the world. I didn't need some caring ear to bring me back. Maybe there was a time when I was like that, but now I was a mature woman of thirty-eight in control of my life, living it the way I wanted to. Damn the psycho babble bullshit.

"So what is this Jimmy like? I Googled him after seeing the video. He's sexy."

"Yes, if you like that sort of thing." I felt like most women would. He had a pretty face and a body built from working in construction. Plus he wore tight blue jeans, t-shirts and a Stetson.

"Seriously? How could you not like it?" Paige wolf whistled. "I bet he could lift you up and throw you all around the bedroom."

"And other places." I couldn't control a smile. My cheeks burned.

"So does a guy with that kind of body know what he's doing?"

I stared out the window at the fields, most harvested, that we zoomed past and let my mind drift away from the case. My sexual awakening, I read that in a novel once and it sounded a lot better than the words I would have chosen, was ... traumatic. I mixed up what sex and love were. By the time I got to Jimmy I wanted things to be a certain way and he was not it. He was tender and loving. That's not what I wanted. Maybe someday, I told myself. I don't know when. He still text me once in a while to ask how I was. If I answered at all it was just a couple words. This morning I got one saying he was in town. He asked if I wanted to grab a coffee. I didn't answer.

"My anger," Paige said after a long time of us riding in silence. "I'd want to get help with my anger. And maybe my self confidence."

"Your anger I can see. The whole fist through a window thing. Why do you think you have low self confidence?"

"Always have. Product of having four gorgeous sisters and a mom always telling me they were better. Prettier."

"Okay, if your sisters are gorgeous what does that make you? You are so beautiful."

"Not compared to them."

"Then they must be pretty hot if they are better looking than you." I kept my eyes on the deer off the side of the highway.

"Guess you would know."

"What?"

Paige glanced at me. "I mean you were a model. I've always felt ugly. I never understood why men were interested in me and I got jealous of women who got what I wanted." She sucked on her bottom lip for a moment. "The self confidence and anger often go hand in hand."

I stared at what was left of a baseball diamond near the Stable. Tall straight poles held up the backstop fence. The diamond was grown over. A pile of logs and tree scraps behind it had yellow barriers around them. It looked sad.

"Maybe my need to prove myself?" I kept staring at the backstop as we drove by. "I have a need to be the best. Maybe I should see somebody about that?"

Chapter 35

WE TURNED FROM THE dirt road onto the driveway and right away saw more vehicles than had been there the last time we visited. The yellow Volkswagen was still there. It was moved over from where it had been the other day, I thought. Slightly closer to the house. There was a new blue Plymouth beside a silver Sunfire I didn't recognize. Four other sedan cars were parked either in the side of the driveway or off on the grass. The pick-up was missing. Paige parked and started writing down license plates.

There were a lot more people walking about this time. I had to wonder if they had been there before but were out of sight. How many people could the house hold? A group quickly moved around the garden. A chainsaw buzzed somewhere. There was a dog watching me. The white hair of it's back was standing up as it waited for me to get out.

Knock. Knock.

Fuck! My skin erupted with tingles. Paige caught her breath.

"Sorry." The woman standing outside my door rocked up on her toes to get closer to the slightly open crack in the window. She pushed back long waves of straw colored hair and smiled with lines forming around her mouth. "I'm Queen. Are you looking for Pony?"

My hand was on my chest. "Yeah."

"I'll take you to him."

I looked at Paige who was studying me. She mouthed the question, "You okay?" Nodding would have to do for a response.

I took a breath before smiling at her and slipping out of the SUV. My hand went to my hip feeling that my Smith and Wesson was still there and made sure my coat was covering it. Today I wore black slacks and a blue and white plaid shirt tucked in at the waist. My jacket was open.

Queen was older than myself by a few years. She had lines around her mouth and dark bags under her eyes. She looked like she had a reason to be at a place like Stable. She was sickly skinny, even in baggy sweatpants and an oversized hoodie. She tied her hair back in a long ponytail. It resembled the same color and texture of dry straw.

"Do you live here?" I hoped my voice sounded casual.

Her ponytail swayed. "I'm a part-timer. Most of the people that live here don't have families or other responsibilities. I have a husband and 3 kids. I can't afford to stay here full time, but I can't afford to let my demons take over my life either."

"How old are your kids?"

"The boys are six and seven and my little girl is two."

"That sounds like a busy life. Do you mind if I ask what brought you here?"

"Like I said, my demons. My boys father." Queen looked forward as she walked. The path was a grown over driveway with the garden on one side and raised beds on the other. The people working at both barely looked up at us. There were some others at a couple of lean-to sheds taking split firewood from a pile and putting it inside. "The asshole was a drug addict. He got me started on them and then left me with two babies and his addictions. They became mine and I thought I could handle it. I couldn't. It took me 5 years to get clean." She looked at the expression on my face and laughed. "Sorry, Pony emphasizes being open and taking claim on your life. It makes you talk more. I own my mistakes."

"So, Pony has helped you?"

"I came here after I was clean, but very tempted to fall back. Without him I would be lost. I've done the rehab and the therapy. I tried them all and I went back to my demons a couple of times and was afraid to go farther down that path. Pony let's us talk, doesn't give us opinions and we work out our issues."

"How much did it cost you?"

"Nothing. Some people can pay money if they want, but for most of us time and sweat equity is all it costs. Are you here looking for healing?" I showed her my police identification. "Doesn't mean you don't have something to heal from." She glanced at Paige who was following at a short distance behind us.

"I don't drink lots and I don't do drugs," I said.

"Those aren't the only addictions." She glanced around, never looking at me.

I counted eight people in total either picking vegetables or digging up the earth. Phoenix stared at me as we walked past. I only recognized a few as being there the first time I came to the Stable. Some looked up and waved. The property seemed larger than I thought with different sheds, areas of woods and an open field area. They had goats and pigs inside one fence, chickens in another. As we got closer to the woods, at what I figured was the edge of the property, the buzzing of a chainsaw got louder. The pick-up was there facing us with its box into the trees. A few people moved around cutting wood or throwing it into the back of the truck. With Queen I counted fourteen on the property in total. My hand grazed my holster as my arms swung. It was a small amount of comfort.

"Corporal," Paige spoke up, "would you mind if I walked around?"

"Yeah, of course." It was all part of the plan.

Queen stopped. "Pony's in there cutting firewood. They say its going to be a cold winter. Best of luck figuring out your problems." She turned and headed back the way we came and the way Paige was walking.

"I don't have ..." What was the point of finishing that sentence? Maybe I did have problems and that was why I came here. I walked toward the woods, my feet squishing into the wet earth.

Pony wielded the chainsaw, cutting logs to size and kicking them out of the way so someone else could grab them and throw them into a pile near the truck. Two men swung axes splitting the thicker pieces in half. One was young looking with blond hair shaved short, I had seen him before. He never looked up at me, but I was sure he knew I was there. The other stopped for a moment as he put a new log on a solid base and winked in my direction. This man's hair was a dark mullet and his beard needed trimming. He rapidly swung an axe hitting his mark. A girl with bright red hair grabbed the chopped wood, watching both men's swings and tossed them into the bed of the pick-up. River was the one throwing the cut logs from where Pony was to the pile waiting to be split. She stopped as I stepped close and slipped a glove off to wipe her forehead with the back of her hand. Something was there on the inside of her right wrist. Pony looked up at her first before noticing me. His shirt was off. Sweat dripped from his hair and down a muscular body. Sawdust stuck to his forearms and chest. He made one more cut before turning the chainsaw off.

"Faryn, didn't think we would be seeing you again." Pony took a few steps to put the chainsaw down and pick up a water bottle. I half expected him to do a slow motion drizzle over his face and chest.

"Kind of cold for no shirt, isn't it?"

His smile showed bright teeth. "Not when you're working. I'm hoping you are here for better reasons than before."

"I wanted to apologize and take you up on a tour of your operation. How are you doing, River?" I silenced my phone two rings in. "Sorry. I should apologize to you too, River." I stepped over a log to get to the young woman and put my hand out. I didn't like using the made up names, but if it made them relax I would do it. "I spoke to your mother again. She won't be looking for you anymore."

Her eyes darted to the leader of the Stable and the others before she put her hand out to take mine. I turned our wrists slightly as we shook so I could see the mark. It was a small tattoo in the shape of a U. No, a horseshoe. Stable? Pony? Horseshoe? Luck? Omega.

"Fuck you." She took her hand back and rubbed it on her side as if she wanted to wipe me away before slipping it back in a glove. "Let her come looking and I'll send her away myself."

"I just said she wasn't going to."

"Okay, ladies." Pony stared at me for a moment. He was studying me. What did he see? Could he see my deception? He blinked. "Well we're all action today. We've had snow fall and melt, so we have to get everything done now. The last of the garden has to harvested and we don't have enough firewood, obviously, so we are cutting some of our wind break. Animals have to be taken care of. The grounds need to be cleaned. Everyone is pitching in."

"Yeah we are," the longer haired chopper called out. Both men leaned on their axes, but all attention was toward me.

"Always good to have backup. Faryn this is Six-String and the short haired gentleman is Coyote and that is Bohemian. Faryn is investigating the death of that woman found a few kilometers away last weekend."

"We all suspects?" Six-String picked his axe up and readied another piece of wood.

"Should you be?" I kept a straight expression for a moment before flashing my best model's smile. "Our investigation is heading in a different direction. I'm here for totally different reasons. Totally personal. So I'm guessing Six-String plays guitar. Coyote?"

"My n-name's Wylie like, like, like the Looney T-tunes guy." He never looked up. He fumbled with his pocket before drawing out a cigarette and flip lighter that popped to life with a flame.

"Be careful with that out here." Pony stared at the younger man who took a long drag before dropping his gaze. He scratched at his collar. Beneath it was the bump of a green tattoo. The top of Omega? How many of them had that tattoo? "Faryn, I'll give you that tour."

Pony motioned for me to turn around and walk back to the gardens. As we walked he pulled a long sleeve shirt on without buttoning it. It was warm today. Autumn in Saskatchewan meant it could be warm one day and snow the next.

Chapter 36

"I'LL ASK YOU NOT TO question everyone about their names," he said when he felt we were far enough from the others. "I can tell you if you really wish to know, but people come to the Stable to shed their sins. They want to make changes in their life, so we don't use their birth names and when someone asks it's as if they are trying to find out who they were."

"I talked to Queen. No, I didn't ask about her name. She says you really helped her."

"I think of it as people helping themselves. I'm just a conduit for them to find a better way."

I fought the urge to roll my eyes. "Either way she gave you credit."

"Here we have our gardens. As you know, we sell things at farmers markets to help pay the bills. Because of the snow we want to get in anything that can be saved. We grow raspberries, tomatoes, gooseberries, onions, shallots, garlic, asparagus, melons, carrots, peas, string beans, zucchini, cucumbers, squash, pumpkins. Did I say cucumbers yet? I'm sure I'm missing things. Beets, did I say beets? There are crab apple trees on the far side and real apple trees in the back corner. We pickle a lot of the veg to keep selling and the fruit we have made jams. We will keep selling eggs, of course, and homemade pasta and some of the gang does arts and crafts that we sell." He stopped close to where the gardening people were. "You know Phoenix and Queen and that is Ranger, Dove, Rain and The Captain.

"That red building in the back is the chicken coup. The Quonset over there is our makeshift barn for the other animals. This bigger building is our garage and work house, I guess you can call it."

"How do you pay for all this? I mean, you say you don't charge anyone and I don't think you'd make enough at the farmers market selling tomatoes and pickled beets to afford all of this." I looked around until I saw Paige talking to two people near the barn. She was close to them as they spoke. Her gaze fell on me and she nodded.

Pony shrugged. "The property belonged to my family. My parents had the mortgage paid off before they died and they left it to me. Government grants, donations. Some of my guests do pay if they can afford it. We live minimalist and as far off the grid as we can. We make sure."

"I'm sorry about your parents. Did that happen after your arrest?"

His mouth opened and he hesitated. "It was a long time ago." Vague.

"Who are your donations from?"

"A variety of people. Most want to remain anonymous. Should we talk about your suspicious nature, Faryn?"

A lawnmower started up across the yard making us both turn. Paige was walking along a fence in close conversation with someone. "I'm a cop because I have a suspicious nature. It helps with the job."

"Are you a cop because you have always had a suspicious nature or are you suspicious of everyone because you are a cop? What makes you suspicious?" Pony headed toward a grassy area which was out of view from everything else. There was a fire pit made from a tractor tire rim with logs and wooden chairs around it. Black ash inside the tire was cold and wet.

"I don't know. I just always remember wondering what angle certain people were playing."

"Which people?"

I shook my head. "Doesn't matter."

Pony spread his arms out. "This is where we do a lot of our healing. We start a good fire and then sit here under the stars discussing what is out of whack and where those feeling came from. Everyone gets to leave and go to bed when they feel they've come to a realization. Some people have sat here well into the next day." He sat on a homemade wooden chair and motioned to another. As soon as I sat he said, "at what age did your father leave?"

"Excuse me?" This time I had to fight the urge to stand and kick him in the face. Maybe I did have issues.

"I'm just assuming that if you always wondered what angle people had that it would be men dating your mother. I'd bet not all of them were nice men. Perhaps they are the reason for your intimacy issues." He looked at me as normally as if what he just said was part of a natural conversation.

I bit down on my tongue until the pain started to make my face shake. I was losing control of this. I wanted to bring up Marta St. John and everything she said, but this was not the place. I was here for my own suspicions. "I'm not here to talk about whatever issues you might think I have."

"Then why are you here? You're not here because you suspect me or any of my guests, you said that earlier, so then I would assume you are here because something is eating away at you. Something you need to get out." He held my gaze. I felt...uneasy. "Let me tell you what I gather from my observations so far. Your father either died or left and your mother...by that look in your eye, I don't think your mother was a good lady herself. You probably played a lot of sports and did a lot of activities growing up to get that feeling of success that you couldn't get from them. You went into police work for that same thing. Every person you help fills you with gratification and fulfillment. You're a grown woman, but your mother still haunts you. You're in a safe place, Faryn. You can talk to me."

"N-no." The last thing I wanted to talk about was my mother. He was completely right, but talking to this man, this suspect, was not an option. How did he know all of that? Was I really that transparent? "Not today." Again he was quiet as he watched me. His eyes took me in. I couldn't help wondering what it would feel like to wake up and have those eyes looking at me from the other side of the bed. As a rapist or a lover? I breathed in deep to stop a tear from falling. I didn't cry. I wasn't that kind of girl. "I should go."

"Have you got everything you came here for?" Pony's tone said he was asking about more than a tour, but was he talking about my emotions or my investigation? How much did he know about me? Where did his information come from?

"Do you mind if I walk around?"

The truck rumbled behind me.

"I do mind, yes. I don't believe you are here for a tour or help or anything as innocent as all that." He leaned back where he sat absently scratching his bare stomach. "You're here to see if I'm a killer. You thought you could play me. Your little friend there is probably asking everyone the question you said you weren't going to ask."

Paige was now talking to yet more people. The gardeners. "If I wanted to talk to you about the murdered girl I would invite you to headquarters. I came here to look around."

"Then invite me."

"Maybe someday soon." I rose from the chair, spun and left him sitting there. I felt eyes on my back. I was sure Pony was watching me. I didn't want to look back at him. I glanced toward the garden and saw Queen and Ranger looking in my direction. Something here didn't feel right. It was a great place if it worked. If it didn't then what was it?

River sat on the hood of my SUV. "Why do you keep coming back here?" She asked as I walked across the driveway. She wasn't happy to have me there. Her left hand played with the buttons of her shirt.

"I came to see what this was all about. I wanted to make sure it was a safe place."

"Why would you care?"

"Something just wasn't sitting right. I wanted to see how this place worked and if Pony was a good guy."

"And what did you find out?"

We stared at each other. I didn't know who this woman was really. I knew who she was when she was born and who she was growing up, but there was a time when that all changed. I had to wonder if she even knew who she was. "That everything is peachy," I said without ever losing her gaze.

River suddenly pushed off the SUV making me step back. "Then don't fucking come back."

"What's your problem?" There's the anger and impulses I was holding back.

"I hate people poking around in my business. I like being left alone."

"None of this is about you and none of it is your business. Unless, of course, you know something about the body."

River's lips curled up at the corner. "You don't know what things are my business."

"Everything okay here, River? Faryn?"

She shook her head as Pony walked up to us. Paige moved to be behind her. "Sure. Just talking. You know, Fare-in, you're so pretty I bet you would look great in pictures."

"Let's go," Pony pushed River's shoulder until she started walking back to the truck. The others were taking the firewood out of the back and throwing it on the pile. I saw them watching. "The police officers are leaving. Have a good day, ladies."

I stood there for a moment watching as Pony strolled our way. Neither of them looked back. River was laughing.

Chapter 37

MY FEET MOVED SWIFTLY across the Major Crimes war room, as we sometimes called it. Delaney looked up from his desk. Bisson's door was closed, but I knew he was in there. Saunders was on the phone. Paige tried to keep pace behind me. She filled me in on everything she got from the Stable members on the ride back to the city while I stared out the window trying to figure out what happened.

I screwed it all up was what happened. Pony played me. He knew what I was doing there. He wasn't going to give me anything.

The phone on my desk rang. I picked it up, "Corporal Steel."

"I timed it right," I knew that voice. I had been talking to him beside a fire pit just over an hour ago.

"What can I help you with, Pony?"

"I just wanted to tell you that I will come to your office for that interview tomorrow. Would 11am work for you?"

"What? Ah, yeah, that would be great. See you then." My stomach twisted in a knot.

Chapter 38

"THIS IS BECOMING A habit," Brandi stepped around me into my house. She had changed from her tactical uniform to sweats and a winter coat.

"Sorry." I took a cursory look outside before shutting and locking the door. "Want a drink? I'm on number three or four."

"Would love to, but I have to get back to the kids. The Man is going out tonight for game night. So," Brandi sat in a chair beside my tiny dining table, "what's the big emergency?"

About ten seconds after getting home I hit Brandi on speed dial. "I need you to come over. I need you to come over right now! I'll explain when you get here." I pushed the hang-up button then grabbed the Captain Morgan from the cupboard. No glass was needed. As the bottle lowered I noticed how quiet my house was.

I tossed a stack of 4x6 photographs with glossy finish on the table making them fan out in front of my friend. In them my head was back in the start of ecstasy, my eyes looked toward the camera. Four hands, two mouths and tongues touched my body.

Brandi stared at them for a while before starting to move them around. She lingered on some a lot longer than I was comfortable with. "I told you, you have a more exciting life than me."

"I could do with boring." I took a drink. "Those were tacked to my front door when I got home. Like some message from a cable guy. I don't know how long they were there. I mean, anyone could have seen them."

Brandi's finger touched the small hole in each picture where a thumb tack had punctured.

"These were on my doorstep last night while people were banging on all my doors and windows." I handed her another stack.

"What are you talking about? When did this happen?"

"Last night. Somebody is fucking screwing with me. Taking pictures through my window, banging -" I took another drink.

"Faryn, did you report this?"

"I talked to a city detective." I turned to the kitchen window. Brandi could usually tell when I was moving around the truth. "I can handle it."

"Right." Brandi knew me well enough to know I was going to be stubborn. I was independent. "Any idea who would do this? Have they said if they wanted anything?"

I offered her the bottle of rum. She shook her head. "I was thinking neighborhood punks at first. Maybe a peeping Tom, but the banging had to be more than one person. This girl said something out at the Stable today. She said she bet I would look great in pictures. It could have meant nothing though." Neighborhood kids wanting to mess with the cop lady was a stronger bet. They wanted me to be on edge. The way River looked at me though. Why would she want to torment me? That would mean others at the Stable would have helped her. Maybe even Pony himself.

Brandi made one stack of the photographs. "Well, if we talk to Bisson and make a report I can lift fingerprints -"

"And have everyone at work know about my sex life?"

"You always say you're not ashamed about it."

My hand hit the countertop. A fork danced on a dirty plate. "I'm not ashamed. It's my business. And I'm not reporting anything to Bisson. He knows I called dispatch about the banging on the doors and stuff. It's probably just a prank that's getting out if hand. I'll deal with it."

Brandi turned the photographs face down. "You, Captain Morgan and the Louisville Slugger on your counter there? You called me for a reason, Faryn. If you won't let me investigate, at least come to my place for the night. Your other friends have to stay here though."

I tapped the wood baseball bat with my fingernails. I had it in my hand as I searched every room and closet when I got home. I even checked under the beds. This was why I called Brandi. I wasn't going to be able to sleep. "I'm fine." Liar.

"I know you're fine, but The Man is going out to play Dungeons and Dragons with his buddies and the kids are going to bed, so I need someone to drink wine with me and watch crime dramas and laugh at what they get wrong. What do you say? You come keep me company. I can dye your hair finally then you can sleep on my couch and I'll drive you home in the morning."

"Can we pick up chicken wings?"

DAY SIX
FRIDAY

Chapter 39

"DID I TELL YOU WHAT I did Wednesday night?" Brandi took our morning coffee from the drive thru attendant and passed them to me.

"Vacuumed in just a pink thong and pasties?" Yes, she had told me what she was doing Wednesday night. She knew she told me. She went to see my ex boyfriend.

"Your Jimmy is so sexy in those tight jeans."

"He's not *my* Jimmy."

"Whatever. He dedicated a song to you."

"Are you fucking kidding me?" I popped the top on my cup and blew in it as I checked myself in the visor mirror. Brandi had added some red auburn to my hair. It took on a richer red. I liked it.

"You think he's the one stalking you?"

"He's not stalking me." I was pretty sure on that. I didn't think it was his style. YouTube videos and phone calls and texting and showing up in my city was his style. "I was stalked when I was seventeen. One of my mother's boyfriends, of all people. He would take pictures of me all the time. He would show up at my sporting events when my mom couldn't be bothered." Nervous laugh. "All of this is bringing back bad memories."

"Do you think this could be that guy?"

"Doubt it. He was practically living with mom and would stare at me as he chewed on a toothpick. Mom found his pictures. He had taken some while I was sleeping. She got mad at me and blamed me for flirting with him." I sipped my Tim Horton's coffee. I had Brandi driving me to the gym in the early morning before taking me back home. She convinced me last night that I should report all if this to Bisson. Step one was telling Emery and Grady. "I ended up installing a chain lock in my bedroom, but then moved out a few weeks later anyway. He continued stalking me for a while. I'd see him outside school and he came to the restaurant I worked at."

"How did it stop?"

"I screamed my head off at him in the restaurant to leave me alone. I don't know if he really stopped or just got better at hiding. I just stopped seeing him." Half truth. There was more to the story, but that was better suited for a psychiatrist's couch than the front of a mini van at 4:30 in the morning.

I counted nine cars in the parking lot, each with a flapping paper held down by a windshield wiper. I was not the only one crazy enough to sweat this early. "Just park in front. I don't see Emery's car." Studio Fitness took up the east end of a small shopping mall where a Zellers department store had been. I watched as several headlights turned into the parking lot. Emery always parked far away from the building so that she had to walk. Practice what you preach, she said.

Last night the conversation always seemed to go back to my life. "What?"

"What?" Brandi sipped her wine.

"You were looking at me instead of at Dr. Reid."

"So I can't look in your direction?"

"You looked like you wanted to ask me something. Spit it out, Brandi."

She took another drink of liquid courage. "You have sex with women."

My head swayed. "Sort of. Was that your question?"

She didn't seem to hear what I said. "What attracts you to a woman?"

"You're not coming on to me are you," I couldn't keep a straight face.

"No. I'm serious. I've only ever been attracted to men, so I'm curious. I saw that woman in the picture. She has a great figure. Is that what gets you hot?"

"Shut up. I'm not really attracted to the women." I shifted how I was sitting and sipped my rum. "I've never had sex with a woman exclusively. I've never fucked one for the sake of fucking. I'm not attracted to the men either." Brandi's mouth was open as she listened. "I'm attracted to the situation."

"But there must be some of them using you. Some sense of that."

I shook my head. "I'm using them. I want wild and crazy sex. I want to be handled by the men and touched by the women. I want to have so many orgasms my legs don't work and I walk funny the next day. But I also don't want to worry about feelings and picking up someone's underwear or whether or not I should feel guilty about eating the last cookie in the bag. I'm attracted to the couple as a whole and what they offer. I've been with a couple like you and The Man."

Brandi put her glass down. "What does that mean? You think we're ugly!"

My eyes rolled. "I mean I've been with average people. I don't need the hard bodies. This couple came along and that's who they are."

Emery parked her car by a far light post like I knew she would. As she started walking I slipped from the minivan and waved as I headed toward her. I could see her smile from where I was. She yelled out something that I couldn't decipher and gave me a big wave. Her pace never changed. She was a woman walking with a purpose wherever she went. Todays outfit was blue and gold leggings and a coat with a fur collar.

Emery stopped. She took slow steps toward a parked Cherokee as if she was expecting and ready for something to jump out at her. The paper on the Jeeps windshield fluttered in the wind. She snatched it without touching the wiper. Her smile was gone. She looked up at me then back at the paper. I glanced at the other cars and stepped toward one.

The paper was a photocopy. A photocopy of a photograph.

Emery ran to each car and tore the papers out. On one the page ripped in half and she had to turn back. Her duffle strap slipped to her elbow. "Faryn, what are these? This is us, isn't it? What are these doing here?"

"I don't know. That's why I'm waiting here, to talk to you about it."

"You knew about this? You knew these would be here? Did you do this?"

"Of course not! And I didn't know these would be here. The other night, did you see the flashes? Somebody took pictures of us and now they're tormenting me." She stared at me as I looked around the parking lot. This was an attack at me, but it could also have been an attack on her. "This is them. Whoever they are."

Emery shook the papers in front of my face. "This is my job, Faryn."

"I know."

"I can't have this here." She pushed the photocopies into my hands. People in the swinger lifestyle didn't want what they enjoyed to be public knowledge. People looked at you differently when they knew.

"I'll fix this," I said with very little confidence. Somebody had to have put these on the cars, but when were they here? How many of these copies were out there? The gym was open 24 hours. They could have put these on the vehicles at any time. At multiple times. How did they know where I worked out? They were following me. I was being watched.

Emery pulled her duffle strap onto her shoulder. "Maybe you shouldn't be here for a while. If people saw this-"

"We have nothing to hide." Bullshit. My life would be hell if this happened at headquarters. I'd become the joke of the month and would be treated different. I touched her arm. She jerked away.

"That's not how other people will see it. This is my reputation." Emery stepped away from me. She stood there a long moment staring at me. She never looked so uncomfortable. Her expression reminded me of my mothers when I tried telling her what her boyfriend was doing. Disbelief. Ashamed.

I turned away giving her the opportunity to go inside without feeling bad.

Chapter 40

I DIDN'T KNOW WHAT to wear. The beige blouse didn't sit over my breasts right, so I took it off and tossed it to the floor. My white bra was in the wash, so that said no to white blouses. I could wear a colored bra, but that would show through. No bra would make the wrong statement. White was too pure anyway. Black was too expected. And what about the bra? Lacey, push-up, plain? I looked in the mirror and took a breath. I was going to interview Pony not go out for a date. I settled on black slacks, turquoise push-up and maroon blouse. The panties didn't match the bra, but it was just work.

I used a little more mascara than normal and Lippie Lingerie pink lip stick. I stared at myself again. Damp hair, dark eyes, moist lips...all set for a day of catching scum bags. My stomach felt like it was doing flips. I hoped it was last nights rum.

"Faryn, I need to speak with you." If I wasn't distracted I might have heard the seriousness in Cheryl's voice as she met me at my truck. Chow-Chow was tucked under her left arm like she was a running back with the pigskin.

I glanced inside my truck before unlocking it and opening the door. "I'm running late, Cheryl."

"What the hell are these pictures?" Her other arm twitched. 4x6 glossy photographs bounced off my chest and soared to the paved driveway. Some slipped under the vehicle. A few landed face down. The ones that were face up showed me with my clothes mostly off. Emery and Grady were enjoying me.

My phone chimed in my coat pocket announcing an email. Ignore.

"How did you get those?"

"Who does this? That's sick filth. Its unnatural." The dog squirmed.

I squatted down and picked up the pictures I could. My gaze fell on the ones under my truck before I stood. "How the hell did you get these, Cheryl?"

Her nostrils flared. Her eyes were spitting fire. "I found this trash in Wendell's bedroom. Who does such, such ... and then takes pictures of it? Do you know what his father will say when I tell him?"

Can I see? "I didn't take the pictures, Cheryl. I obviously didn't. You can tell they were taken through my window. I don't know who took them."

"Oh seriously? You honestly expect anyone to believe you did this fifty shades stuff out in the open and didn't know someone was taking pictures? In a couple of them you are looking right at the camera. I'm not stupid, Faryn. Why would these be out there? Why would Wendell have them? You're disgusting."

"Fuck you Ms. High and Mighty. Maybe your pervert son took the pictures."

I didn't see her hand. Ms. High and Mighty balled up a fist and fired it right at my face. The knuckles glanced my cheek bone and headed into the left eye. I felt diamonds from her rings cut into my flesh. My feet stumbled. Red heat fired in my cheekbone. Her fist fit perfectly in the socket. The eye pulsed with pain. My hand covered it. I felt something wet under my palm. It ran down my cheek.

"Fuck you!" I heard Cheryl's shoes click down the driveway. Chow-Chow yipped. "Stay away from my boy." She didn't utter until she was across the street then, "fuck you," was directed back at me.

Chapter 41

"ARE YOU AT WORK YET?"

I had just parked behind headquarters when Brandi called. I still felt the radiating pain from the punch and rings. "What? No, I just pulled in."

"Have you checked your work email yet?"

"Brandi, I'm not in the mood."

"Have you checked it?" Her tone stabbed.

"My work email? No, why?"

"Youmightwanttocheckit!" Her words all blended into one fast splash. I had to ask her to repeat herself. "Before you go inside. Like, right now."

"Okay, hold on I'll go inside and check." I opened the truck door.

"No!" I closed the door. "Check it on your phone. About an hour ago an email was sent out. It looks like it was sent to just about everyone in the division. Even the higher ups in Ottawa. You'll want to take a look."

Give me a minute." I wanted to get inside and get myself ready for Pony. I put Brandi on speaker and touched the email icon. The inbox popped up.

There were a dozen new emails since I last checked it, but the one she was talking about stuck out. It had my name in the subject. Corporal Faryn Steel Behind Closed Doors. The email address was not from another officer. It had some letters and numbers, she666ri78f99f@gmail.com. It had to have passed our virus scans. My thumb touched the email. I expected words. Instead a picture appeared on my phone screen. It was me looking toward the camera.

A man was down on his knees in front of me with his face buried between my thighs, eating me as if he was starving, and a woman had one of my breasts in her mouth. In the next picture I had a mouthful of tit. Then I was hanging onto a dining chair as Grady pushed himself in me from behind. From the camera view you couldn't see Emery, but she had the best seat for the show. Oh. My. God.

"OhmyGod! These went to everyone?" My body vibrated. There was no way to stop this.

"I know you always say you aren't ashamed of your lifestyle, but that was when nobody knew. You showed me last night, but an email to everyone? I mean, wow. I checked who they were sent to. Saunders, Delaney, Bisson, everyone."

"Oh my God. What the hell is happening to me? Someone's trying to ruin my career. Whose doing this?"

"You're not ruined."

Spittle flew from my lips and splashed against the steering wheel.

"You're not in a good place, but not ruined. I don't see you getting fired over this, at least. There have been worse scandals and those officers survived. You'll have to deal with a lot of talk and whispers behind your back probably. It's harassment. They can't fire you for being harassed."

I flipped back through the pictures and stopped on the second one. I had given up on the camera and given into what was happening, grasping Emery's breasts and tugging on a nipple. It was her eyes that caught me. She was excited and in the moment. This time she was staring at the camera. She *must* have seen the flash. That must have been why she shrunk down and stayed out of view until we went to the bedroom. She knew there was a camera. She never said anything then or this morning. I got to the one with Grady in me. This time he stared at the window. He knew. They both knew. Was it their game?

"Shit, I have to go inside." I had to deal with it head on. That was the only choice. "Pony will be here at eleven. I'm going to see if he'll give a blood sample, so I might need you." I put my phone up to my ear and walked toward the back door of the building.

"You know it'll take a few days for a DNA match, right?"

"Yes, but he probably won't know that. Just be ready."

Now I had more to do than just be nervous.

Chapter 42

I HAD GRABBED MY POLICE ball cap from the backseat and pulled it down low with the bill covering my face before walking into HQ and heading straight to Major Crimes. People said, good morning, but I ignored them and made a line to my desk. I fell into my chair. Bisson's office door was closed. Ottawa was one hour ahead of us. They were already working. They had all seen that email and other emails had to have been sent in reply. At any moment someone was going to mention it.

"Hey, Faryn." Charles Delaney rested his hip against my deck. Prick.

I looked up at him quickly then focused on Bisson's door. "Go away Chuck." My mind was off my game. This was the last person I wanted to talk to.

"Jesus, what happened to your eye?"

Driving to work I pressed napkins from an old fast food bag against the cuts. There were three of them beside my left eye. Pain still pulsed out from the socket bone. "Nothing. I fell."

"Looks like you got punched."

"Nope."

"I looked into your shoe thing and the house invasions. Shoes were missing in most of them. Lots of stuff was missing." His voice sounded smug.

"Okay, thanks." Go away.

"I like the hair color. Sexy." He licked and smacked his lips. "I saw your email," Delaney had that cocky asshole tone in his voice. His hip bounced against my desk again making the whole thing move.

"It wasn't my email." Of course he would be the first one to say something. My teeth squeezed down on my bottom lip. The pain reminded me to stay calm.

"Whatever. That was you right?" He glanced around. His voice went quiet. "So are you, like, a swinger?"

I didn't move. I didn't want these people knowing about my life. It wasn't traditional. It wasn't what people expected. I didn't know if it would always be that way, but that was my decision for the time being. Most people had their opinion and in this day and age they felt they had a right to impose them on you.

Delaney squatted down so that his arm rested on the top of my desk. His hand moved close to mine. "The wife and I have been dipping our toes in that lifestyle, so to speak."

"Don't do it."

"Come on, we've been looking for a woman to join us. What are they called, unicorns? A mythical woman that enjoys both men and women, but also might not exist. It's obviously not your first time." His finger caressed a line on the back of my hand.

I suddenly got that metallic taste of blood in my mouth as my teeth pressed into my lip. My neck muscles were all tight. I wanted to get up and run away. Through clenched teeth I said, "If you want to keep using that finger to play with your own asshole you're going to get up and walk the fuck away from me." I never raised my tone. A chill crept up my back from the sound of my own smoky voice. Delaney raised his finger but still didn't move.

"Don't get all mad at me because your naked nips are on everyone's computer."

Breathe Faryn. I bit hard on my lower lip as I turned and stared at him. "I don't care that my naked body is everywhere. I've modeled nude. I can send you all the nudes you want. I can't stand the fact that the world thinks a bare nipple is going to end everything. You probably sucked on you mothers fucking nips. What I'm pissed about is someone sharing my personal fucking business!"

"Steel, in my office." Bisson marched across the room.

"Did I just save you or Delaney." He sat down behind his desk.

Good question. "Little of both, I think. I assume you saw an email about me? I hope you know I had nothing to do with that. I was in my private home after hours. I didn't know someone was outside my house taking pictures and by the time I did I, we, it had gone too far. You know how things can be."

He smiled beneath his moustache. "Hard to stop a train once its started. I've already had phone conversation about this. The other people in the picture were of legal age. We are all certain you did not intend for these pictures to get out. Though I may not agree with what you are doing in them, there is nothing we can hold against you. If you had nothing to do with the pictures or email, who did?"

I stayed standing and tried not to look in his eyes. My heart raced. "I don't know, Sir. It might have something to do with what happened the other night. The people banging on my door and windows. They left copies of the pictures. My neighbors son had copies too. I asked Greg Vista about reports in my area, but he said there were none.

"Did you make an official report?" The chair creaked as he leaned back.

"No, not yet."

"Do it then. And tell Vista I want to be copied on it." I frowned and he smiled. "That should make sure you actually report it."

"I can handle it."

Bisson made a hum noise. "What happened to your eye? What would have happened to Chuck if I didn't come along?"

"I wanted to hit Delaney plenty of times in the past and still haven't." I wanted him to go away and couldn't find the words. He made me feel small. Dirty. I was an angry child and teenager and some of it spilled over into adulthood with all those feelings of not being worth anything lingering in the back of my mind. It made for a work record with a lot of write-ups. "He's just a prick talking out his fantasy that's never going to happen. I've dealt with worse."

"Under your command? If anyone says or does anything, you send them to me. Triangle meeting in twenty minutes."

"Everything okay?" Brandi got up from my chair. She looked more worried and tired than when she dropped me off at home. "What happened to your eye?"

I dropped to me chair. "If you mean already being propositioned this morning, sure, I'm doing okay."

"What? By who?"

"Someone wanting me to join him and his wife for fun and games. Doesn't matter. Bisson says he has my back. Wants me to report it to Vista with city police."

"Good plan. And the eye?" I shrugged off the question. She seemed okay with that. "I wanted to talk to you about the email."

"Morning guys," Paige dropped a purse beside the desk she had been using. She got in her chair and wheeled it close to me. "Faryn, I saw that email. Oh my God, right."

"You saw it?" Brandi sipped coffee.

"Yes. Why would something like that go out?"

"Don't know. What's wrong with you?" My shoe tapped Brandi's boot. She had been staring in Paige's direction. She blinked fast and put her attention on me.

"Nothing. Can I talk to you about something?"

Bisson stepped out of his office and headed for the meeting room.

"Meeting time. It can wait, right?"

Brandi checked her phone. "I have a scene."

"Then we'll talk later. Paige, let's go."

Chapter 43

THE DESK PHONE CALLER ID said it was the front desk calling.

"Hey Eddy, what is it?"

"You have a visitor."

I hung up. The clock said it was 10:30 am. "He's early. Paige, come with me. We'll show force." I grabbed my tablet.

Saunders had explained during the Triangle meeting that a few tips had come in from the public since the release of the security video Jane Doe picture. Paige and I spent the morning calling those that called in. I wasn't sure what to make of any of it. People didn't want to believe their friends or loved ones were murdered, so only a few said they knew who the woman was. The picture we released was grainy and others in it had to be blurred out which meant it could have been anyone. It could have been me. Other's said they had been at the Greek and wanted to tell what they saw. It was all boiling down to nothing.

Major Crimes was on the second floor and down two hallways from the front doors. Interviewing someone was about control. At the Stable Pony had control. Today he was mine. This was my turf. Except as we walked down the hallway my eyes were focused on the floor so I didn't have to see the way people were looking at me.

When people came into the police station they were met with a small lobby that had one bench and a glass case holding pictures and awards of the detachment. Opposite the front door was a booth with a security guard inside. He had to call to the departments and find out if these people could go in or not. Eddy pushed the button to unlock the door for the two of us to enter.

Standing in front of the display case was a man with black and silver hair under a baseball cap, broad shoulders and a muscular body. He wore blue jeans and a t-shirt that hugged his biceps. On his feet were work boots. He played the part of a country singer all the time.

"Jimmy? What are you doing here?" I felt Paige squeeze in behind me.

Jimmy nodded toward me with his hard jaw. Okay, for a single woman the country singer looked like a great catch. "You don't see me for how long and that's the first thing you say to me? Faryn, you texted me. I would rather see you than text you back, so I came here. You're not that hard of a person to find, right."

My arms crossed in front of me. I felt the anger building inside me. "No, I mean what the hell are you doing here in Saskatoon? You're supposed to be on the West coast not here."

"I go where the music takes me."

"Oh shut up."

Paige made a noise behind me.

"I'm touring, Faryn. I'm trying to sell music, get a deal, make a go of it. What's your problem?"

I stared into his eyes for a moment hoping he would see the problem. I saw he was looking at my injury. "My problem is a YouTube video that has my personal pictures on it."

"They're your modeling pictures."

"Not all of them! Some of them were very personal."

"You model, Faryn. Your pictures are easy to find. The photographer has them on Instagram for Christ sake. In fact, I was hoping you would be flattered that I made the video. I dedicate a song to you on every set, you know." Jimmy reached out and rubbed his hand along my upper arm. I glanced down at it, but didn't move. Our thing together had taken place over a few months. My last feeble attempt to have an actual relationship. "I still care about you. I want you to see that."

"Do you really want to go back over our relationship right now?" I don't know what he remembered about it, but what I recalled was the loud fights and worse. He really didn't like that I would never spend the entire night at his place and didn't trust why. For a moment I sucked on my bottom lip. "How long have you been in town?"

His hand dropped. "A few days. I was afraid to call. I went by your house once."

"Were you outside my house Tuesday night with a camera?"

"What? What are you talking about?"

"You know what I'm talking about." The anger was building. "Tuesday night, were you outside my house," the door behind him opened, "taking pictures of me and my-"

"You and your what?" Spit flew from his lip hitting my ear. "Your fuck buddies? This about you and your *alternative lifestyle?*" He leaned back and made air quotes on the word alternative like it was something disgusting. "You go screw whoever you want to, go fuck your married couples, but leave me out of your damn fantasies."

I had stopped listening to Jimmy and was staring at the men standing behind him. Pony's thin lips showed little expression. He stared past the country singer to me. Another man stood behind him. I focused again on Jimmy and stepped close. "You were never part of my damn fantasies. That's why I dumped your ass. You sure as fuck aren't in them now. Get out of here."

He backed away keeping his gaze on me. "This isn't over, Faryn."

"Suck my cock, Jimmy!"

"It's not over," he hit the door hard as he stormed out.

Chapter 44

"SEEMS LIKE A NICE GUY," Pony said with a smile.

I turned to Paige who had a large smile on her face. "Can you go continue what we were doing? We will be in the interview room."

"This is Vern Chambers, my lawyer."

"Nice to meet you, Corporal Steel." The lawyer had bright teeth. His face was clean shaven except for the starts of a porno moustache. Movember. The hand that didn't reach out to shake mine held onto a leather case. His charcoal suit looked more expensive than my truck.

I shook his hand but didn't speak to him. Real interviews between the police and suspects was not like in American crime dramas. In my experience it was actually unusual for someone to show up with a lawyer. Most people would call one and get advice on what to talk about or to say. Did Pony having a lawyer mean something? "You brought a lawyer. Are you worried?"

"My client has the right to have representation. Especially to protect his innocence."

"How can someone who doesn't charge his clients afford a lawyer like yourself?"

"He saved my wife. I believe you met her." Queen. "Are we going to stand here in the lobby doing this?"

"This is what it takes to get you not to talk?" I stared into Pony's eyes. He gazed into mine. The man behind him waited a moment before looking at his wristwatch and clearing his throat. "Follow me."

"Did you want to talk about what just happened with your friend," Pony walked more at my side.

My eyes rolled back. "That didn't last. Not really. It's nothing to waste time on."

"Are you sure? It must be quite embarrassing to have your friend blow up like that in front of your coworkers. Listening to people is what I do."

"You're not my therapist, thanks."

"Do you have a therapist?"

"Right in here." Pony wore a sport coat over a plaid shirt, the cuffs of the shirt stuck out the cuffs of the jacket, and jeans over $10 sneakers. Where Jimmy looked like the perfect image of a country guy, Pony resembled a Bohemian intellectual. He didn't look like a killer. "Somebody will come in in a minute for a DNA sample. That okay?"

"No, it's not," Vern Chambers spoke quickly. He stood beside the table as his client sat down. "Unless you have a warrant that's not happening."

"So this is how this is going to be?" I looked at Pony when I spoke. He stared back at me.

"Corporal, you can direct your questions to me."

I took a breath. "Have a seat, Mr. Chambers." This time I stared at the lawyer until he sat next to his client. He took a yellow legal pad from his case. He tapped a pen against it over and over.

It was a plain room with beige painted walls, a map of the city on one wall and a table and four chairs at the far end. There was a window looking out at the hallway. The blinds were closed. I pressed record on a video camera that sat up on a tripod. After stating the date I said, "this is Corporal Faryn Steel questioning Randall Poniatowski, aka Pony. Also present is the attorney Vern Chambers."

"What exactly do you think I've done, Faryn?" Pony knew I was taking the power from his lawyer. This was his way of trying to take it back. He knew the game. "Do you want me to tell you where I was Saturday night again and give you a list of witnesses?"

"We'll get to that in a bit. Do you know a woman named, Naomi Fuller?"

"Don't answer that," the lawyer raised his voice. "What is all this about, Faryn?"

"Are we that familiar, Mr. Chambers? I don't think so." I stared at him until his pen stopped tapping. "I believe your client may have some knowledge about events from Saturday night as well as several incidents over the past year and a half."

"Naomi has nothing to do with Saturday."

Chambers tapped Pony's arm to tell him to be quiet.

"Background questions. Do you know her?"

Pony leaned back in the chair. He pulled his hand away from Chambers. "Right. She said you were asking questions about me. We hung out a few times. We had some fun. I wish I could go back to that night she was hurt and maybe drive her home or walk her, anything to keep her safe, however it was impossible to know what would happen at the time."

"So you know she was attacked. Do you admit to having sex with her that evening?"

"Earlier in the bar bathroom, yes. It might sound disgusting to you, but with her one foot up on the toilet seat it made everything a little tighter from behind." We both smiled at the lawyers sigh. "But then you have your own depravity, so maybe you don't find it disgusting." Pony's head tilted. "Have you ever had sex in a public bathroom, Faryn?" Yes.

The way he openly talked about the sex act set me back a second. "You don't find it funny that she got attacked shortly after being with you?"

His finger drummed. "Funny isn't the word I would use. That shouldn't happen to anyone and now she connects being with me with that night. I haven't even seen Naomi since that night. She called me to let me know that you talked to her because she wanted me to be prepared for your questions. I help people, both in and out of the Stable, and knowing I can't help someone is heartbreaking. Did you change your hair colour?"

On the one hand I was surprised he noticed, but on the other I wanted to grab him by his collar. "What about Marta St. John? Do you know her?"

"Faryn, why don't you ask me questions you don't know the answers to?" He brushed the hair away from his face running his fingers through it. He looked at his hand and shook a loose strand into the air. "Marta came to the Stable because of a personal problem. We talked a lot, spent time together and I was able to make her feel better and have more confidence in herself. We then started a relationship of sorts. I can't say it really ended. We just stopped seeing each other."

"What do you know about her attack?"

"Again, its heartbreaking. Women should not have to live a life where that could happen."

"What are you two talking about," Chambers asked.

"What do you make of both women you had relationships with being attacked?" I turned a pen with my fingers.

"Lots of women get attacked. I don't know all of them. And I wouldn't call Naomi and myself a relationship."

"Fuck buddies? Both women had sex with you and then later were attacked. That's pretty shitty."

Pony took a deep breath and let it out through his nose. He looked at his lawyer who was shaking his head.

"Remember when I said we all have our demons? Mine is that. I'm addicted to sex." His hand raised. "Safe, consensual sex. I like to fuck. It doesn't really matter where or with who. If there's an attraction I'll want it to happen."

"So you help people with addictions, but you yourself are addicted to sex."

"I talk people who want to be saved down from their own addictions, however this is not one I am willing to give up. I go to the Greek often looking for that high."

"Maybe that high wasn't high enough."

"You don't need to answer these questions, Pony." Chambers was taking notes.

Pony raised his hand to quiet the lawyer. His gaze didn't leave me. "Addicted to sex is the polite way of saying it. I want to fuck ... Faryn. My partners want it as much as I do. It is always consensual. A good fuck is only great if everyone is into it."

Don't squirm. Don't squirm. I couldn't argue with him there. "Maybe having a willing partner didn't excite you enough anymore and you needed to take it."

"Come on now, Corporal."

"I didn't rape those women. I don't hurt people."

"But yet, you brand the people at the Stable."

His brow furrowed. "What are you talking about?"

"I saw a few at the Stable with the same horseshoe tattoo. Are you branding them into your inner circle?"

"Now you're getting ridiculous." Chambers dropped his pen in exasperation as he leaned back.

"I never made anyone to get a tattoo."

"Why do they have the same tattoo? I'm really curious."

"You'll have to talk to them then."

"I will do that. Why don't we talk about Saturday."

The lawyer cleared his throat and took up his pen. "My client informed you what he had done the night in question."

"Yes. What was that again?"

Pony sighed. His fingers stopped drumming and his eyes left me. "I was driving around. Some of the others were with me."

"Who was that?"

"River, Coyote, Dove."

I wrote their names down. "All you did was drive around, correct?"

"Pony answered that question."

I grinned as I opened a file on my tablet. I pressed play on a video and held it so the two of them could see. "Could you tell me, if you were just driving around then why are you on this security video from the Greek? As you can see its date stamped for Saturday night. This is you right?"

The video showed the pub with lots of people moving around. Pony was there with his people in the same corner I saw him in. A woman in a brown dress walked across the room winding through all the tables. She had long brown hair. I paused the video.

Pony's mouth was open. He leaned into the tablet staring at the paused picture. His lawyer shook his head.

"Are you going to tell me the truth now?"

"I wasn't there. I don't remember being there at all. I swear I wasn't."

"Let's cut through the, were you there questions. You were at the Greek Saturday. You spoke to this woman. It's right fucking here. Who is she?"

Vern Chambers tugged on Pony's jacket and pulled him toward him. "Don't say a word until we can talk about this." He turned to me. "Can I have a few moments with my client?"

I paused for a moment before standing and turning the video camera off. By law the person being interviewed and their lawyer had the right to speak in privacy. It broke up where I was going in the interview, but I didn't have a choice. I stared at Pony as I picked up the tablet. His eyes were wet.

Chapter 45

"HOW'S IT GOING?" SAUNDERS glanced at the interview room door. I leaned on the wall across from it, where I had been for fifteen minutes, chewing ice from a paper cup. I just shrugged my shoulders and grunted. "What? Did he bring a lawyer?"

"Vern Chambers," I said around a cube.

"Expensive."

"Pro bono, I think. His wife goes to the Stable. Recovering drug addict. As soon as I brought up the security video he asked for a pow wow. Probably won't say another word to me."

Saunders looked at my face. "Want to talk about that?"

I popped another cube in my mouth.

"Well, I have something you might like. We got a warrant to get Pony's DNA sample. Someone from Ident will be here soon to get it. Keep him here until they show up."

I nodded. "He admits to knowing Naomi and Marta and having sex with them. Still says he wasn't at the Greek on Saturday though. Seemed stunned when I showed him the video."

"What if he's not a DNA match?"

A couple of constables walked down the hallway passing the two of us. They both turned back and looked at me a few strides away. They turned away as soon as they saw me looking.

"Then I've wasted all this time. It's going to match. It has to."

Saunders was staring after the constables. "Don't worry about that email either. It'll all blow over."

"I can deal with it. Can you call the Wakaw detachment and have them go to the Stable. I want three people brought in for interviews. Pony says he was with them Saturday night." I wrote the names down for him.

"Consider it done."

Chapter 46

"SHALL WE CONTINUE?" I put my cup of ice and tablet on the table but stayed standing.

"My client has nothing more to say."

I glanced at the lawyer before settling my gaze on Pony. One, two, three. "What was her name?" Four, five, six.

My mother always counted to ten when she was mad at me or I wasn't doing what she thought I should be doing. Before she got to seven she would get frustrated, grab whatever was closest and side arm it at my head. The woman could have been a relief pitcher for the Toronto Blue Jays.

"I don't know."

Chambers put his hand on Pony's shoulder and spoke close to his ear. "Remember what I said."

"Oh come on, Pony. I hate it when people say they don't know anything. It usually means they don't want to tell me."

"Or it means, I don't know." His voice took a whiney pitch. "I don't remember being there. Don't look at me like that. I see that I was there, but I don't remember being there." Pony lost his composure. His lawyers head was continuously shaking. His voice had changed, there was sweat forming on his brow. He was twitchy. He was confused.

"Here's what I think happened. You chatted up a woman at the Greek and had sloppy drunk sex with her in the car that you told me was stolen. You decided to take her. I don't know why yet. Just her unlucky day. Maybe she passed out. Somewhere along the way she came to. What happened next? I know the car got stuck. Did she

199

jump out and run? Did you give chase with the shotgun in hand? Was it an accident?" I had to step around the subject to get him to admit what happened. First he could admit it and then we could get to the woman's trauma.

"I don't know."

"You keep saying that."

"Pony, stop talking."

"I keep saying it because I don't know. I can't tell you what I can't remember." He stared at the tablet as if that one paused moment of him in the bar would tell him what he said he could not remember.

I sunk down into the chair opposite. "Let's back it up then, Pony. You said sex was your demon or whatever. Is alcohol one too?"

"No."

"But it was this time."

"I don't know."

"Drugs?"

"I do take drugs."

"Did you this time?"

"What? No. I don't know."

It was the classic amnesia defence that most guilty people took when they didn't want to admit to themselves what they had done. My mother was like that. The next day, hours later, the next sentence, she would forget however she had punished me for whatever she thought I had done. My life was full of people saying they didn't know. Because of my life and job I didn't believe any of them. "Why don't we go over what you did on Saturday."

"This isn't going to solve anything, Corporal."

"Mr. Chambers, you are here to advise your client. I will do what my job requires without your suggestions."

"Then my advice to my client is to stop talking."

A smirk crossed my lips. "Is telling me what he did during his day really going to incriminate him?"

The two of them looked at each other and exchanged nods. "A few of us went to the Farmers Market in Saskatoon," Pony started.

"Who was with you?"

"This time it was Phoenix, Six-String, Ranger. Queen dropped by during the market."

"How did you get there?"

"The Volkswagen and pick-up."

"Not the Neon?"

"Faryn, we told you it was stolen three weeks ago."

I checked the time. "What did you do after the market?"

Pony rubbed his temples. "We went home. Coyote had supper made. After that," he stared at me though I wasn't sure if he was looking at me, "someone suggested going out. River, Sheriff, Coyote, I don't remember. I do remember they suggested going for a drive. Can I have some water?"

"Who is Sheriff? I haven't heard that name yet."

"What?" He looked around the room for a moment. "I can't talk about my clients. You will have to talk to, um, him."

"Why don't we talk more about Saturday night then? Maybe I can help you remember."

Pony blinked and stared at me. "Can I have a glass of water, please?"

Chambers wrapped on the table. "We are done here. Pony, let's go."

There was a knock on the door before it opened and someone walked in. "Are you ready for me?" Corporal Olivier Faucher did not wait for an answer as he stepped inside the room.

"What's this?" Chambers took the paper the officer handed him.

"Corporal Faucher is here to serve a warrant for Pony's DNA sample."

The lawyer read the paper. He looked up at his client and nodded. One for me.

Chapter 47

"THIS WAS A COMPLETE violation of my client's rights."

"Seriously," I led the way down the hallway toward the front door, "he doesn't let you use his real name either?" The more I smiled the madder the lawyer got. "Do you get to use your wife's real name?"

"So glad I can entertain you, Corporal."

Pony was quiet as we walked. He didn't speak again after Faucher came in the room. I had him.

I knocked on the door and Eddy buzzed us into the lobby. Paige was in there speaking to a woman. They both stopped talking as we walked in.

"Here she is. This is Corporal Faryn Steel. She's running the investigation into what happened Saturday night."

The woman stood a little taller than Paige. She had long brown hair which fell loose over her shoulders. Chocolate eyes looked at me and the men. She wore a black coat with fake fur on the hood. A brown dress was draped over one arm. The two men stepped around me, but only Pony's eyes lingered on her. Perve. Slut.

Why was there no slang name for a man that liked to fuck around?

The woman put her hand out. "I'm the woman you are looking for. Brown dress at the Greek Saturday night."

"What is this?" Chambers stopped moving so fast Pony had to step around him.

"Sorry," Paige said.

"Thank you, gentlemen. I'll be in touch." I stepped between the men and the women. The lawyer had the right question, what was this? Our victim was the woman in the video. How could this be that woman?

Chambers put his arms up. His brief case slapped his elbow. "Wait a minute, Corporal. This is the woman from the security video you said was dead. Would you like to explain how my client is a suspect in her death if she is obviously alive?"

I looked in his direction and held his gaze as my mind went crazy. "The woman in the morgue is obviously dead and your client is still my primary suspect."

"So, you don't even have a name for your victim? If there's no victim, there's no crime!" Spittle formed on the lawyer's lips.

I stepped close so I didn't have to yell back. "Do you want to go down to the fucking morgue and look at the body? Don't tell me that no fucking crime happened."

"Then do your job, Corporal."

Chapter 48

"WHAT'S YOUR NAME?"

"Eva Binion."

"And you were at the Greek Brew Pub on Saturday?"

"Yes."

"And you were wearing this brown dress?" It was now draped over the table in the interview room. It was close to the one taken from the body. So close they could have been from the same rack.

The room smelled of Pony. Distracting.

"Yes."

Six days had gone by since the woman we called Jane Doe has lost her life in a field. Six days of being focused on this woman being at a bar and running into Pony. Right here was someone telling me it was a waste of time. Eva and Jane Doe both had long dark hair. In the out of focus security video it could have been either of them walking through the crowded pub. It wasn't either one though. It was this one! Eva Binion, a living and breathing woman.

You want to solve a case in the first two days if you can. Witnesses, evidence, VICTIM IDENTIFICATION, suspects and then getting the admission of guilt. I had missing parts. I latched onto past forensic evidence and got tunnel vision. Bisson warned me not to fixate on one suspect. I screwed up.

"Um, did you know either of the men you saw me with?"

Eva shook her head. Her stupid hair flopped around. "No. The one with the glasses looked familiar. I probably saw him around somewhere."

So this is what a dead end looked like. I could actually see the entire case going cold. "Saturday night you were at the Greek." Duh. "Were you there alone? With friends?"

"My sister and her husband and a couple friends. We haven't been out in a while, so we went. I didn't know it would be this big of a deal. Was I a witness to something?"

"To be honest, we thought the woman in the video was our victim."

"But it's me."

"Yeah, well, we thought it was the young woman whose body was found on Sunday. We were hoping someone would come forward knowing who she was."

"Oh my God. That could have been me."

"I'm glad it wasn't you," her facial expression had changed to stunned fear, "but now I have a lot more work to do."

"Now I feel bad." Her face said she was more happy than sad.

I got to my feet. "Seriously, you don't have to. I have to get back to work, so I'll walk you out."

"Of course. When I first heard you were looking for someone in a brown dress I wasn't sure if you meant me or the other woman. Then I saw the picture of the video."

"Other woman? What other woman?" I stopped Eva before opening the door.

Eva stared at me for a moment. "There was another woman outside the pub that had a dress almost the same as mine."

"Did she go inside?" There was only one brown dress wearing woman on the security video.

Her face scrunched up. "I don't think so. We were going in and her friends and her were talking to the bouncer. I'm pretty sure the people she was with came in right behind me."

I played the video on my tablet and Eva pointed out five women she said were with the other woman in a brown dress. That woman never went in. My insides twisted. There was still a chance that I was right. The pieces were there.

Chapter 49

"THANKS FOR COMING IN, River."

"Did I have a choice?" She looked up at me from where she sat behind the small table. "What the hell happened to your face? You're not pretty as a picture anymore."

All three of the Stable members were put in separate interview rooms. I wanted to go to the Greek and talk to the bouncer, but these three had to come first.

River was pissed off, of course. She felt like life owed her and she wanted me to play her game. Only I wasn't playing. There was time later to drill her on what she knew about the pictures.

"Would you like me to call your mom and tell her you're here? Maybe she can bring your daughter to see you."

I got a hard stare in reply.

I pointed to the tattoo on her wrist. "What does that mean? I've seen it on a few at the Stable."

She shrugged. "Coincidence."

"Do you want to know what the police think about coincidence?" I took a sip of coffee.

Her head dropped to one shoulder. "What do they think about one of their own being a porn queen?"

I almost choked. "Excuse me?"

"I saw pictures of you." In her eyes I could see she was having a good time. "You're all over the internet screwing a couple. What are their names?"

I pushed my mug away. My breaths came fast. "I thought you didn't have access to the web." I was all over the internet? Strangers were seeing those pictures? People I knew could be seeing them. I had to find them. I had to find them now!

River looked away from me. "Pony can't watch all of us every minute of the day. Look, are we here for a reason?"

Again, the pictures would have to wait. I got my breathing under control. "Let's talk about Saturday."

Chapter 50

"CAN YOU STATE YOUR name for the recording?"

The man across the table rubbed the stubble on his head. His gaze stayed locked on the tabletop. "C-Coyote."

"Your real name and louder for the video, please."

He flinched toward the camera. "W-w-w-wylie T-teller."

"Like Wylie Coyote? Cute." He was nervous, so I tried to make my voice as friendly as I could to make him comfortable.

"Yeah, I guess. O-only spelled different."

"You prefer, Coyote, don't you?"

"Pony likes it."

"Do you like Pony?"

Coyote lifted his shoulders. It took a couple breaths before they dropped. "I, I like him. He's helped me. He is helping me."

"He seems to have helped a lot of people."

Coyote cracked his knuckles. He began pushing his finger knuckles into the palm of his hand making the joints pop.

"That's what he does, right? Do you mind me asking why you are at the Stable?"

He raised his blue eyes to meet mine. He looked frightened. "P-p-pony's helping me with my sh-shyness. I, I, I was afraid of everything. He helps me get out and around people a-and helping me build my confidence."

"You don't seem that confident right now."

I actually got a smile. "You i-i-i-intimidate me."

"The police intimidate you?"

211

He pulled his green camouflage jacket tight around him. He glanced at me quickly and said, "no."

"The tattoo on your neck," as I pointed at it he turned so it was hidden in his collar, "Omega, right? A neck tattoo seems out of place on you."

He put his hand over it. "I, I, I thought it would make me look tough."

"Does it mean anything?"

His shoulders raised. "I don't know. I saw it on someone and liked it, I, I guess."

"Pony didn't tell you to do it? Do you regret getting it?"

"I, I do not regret the things I've done, but those I, I did not do."

If these three were going to tell me the story of going for a drive and not about being at the brew pub, I was going to have to make one break and this one was going to be it. He was the weak link. He was intimidated whether it was by me or what I represented, it didn't matter. First I had to find out what story they were going to tell and then I had to find out what part they played in the murder.

"I want to talk about last Saturday. Can we do that?"

Chapter 51

"HEATHER TURTLE, BUT I go by Dove."

"Turtle Dove, cute."

"It was Pony's idea." Her blond hair was cut straight across her shoulders. Letting it grow out? I noticed her thighs when she walked in. They were thick with muscle inside leggings. She had extra piercings in her ears. There was a mole next to one eye and her nose looked crooked. I don't think it was always that way.

"So you don't seem like an addict. What brought you to the Stable, if you don't mind me asking." I couldn't see any tattoo, but that didn't mean anything. Maybe an omega tramp stamp. The end of everything right above her butt. How poetic.

Dove nibbled her bottom lip. "I don't mind. Talking about it takes away their power. That's what Pony says. I have PTSD from being attacked."

"Oh, I'm sorry."

She leaned back and raised her chin. "Someone gave me a drug that took away my free will and most of the memories of that night, but I know what happened." She stared off for a moment before continuing. "One of them took pictures of them raping me and posted them online. I couldn't remember who they were and their faces weren't in the pictures. There was four of them." She laced her fingers together in front of her, calm as could be. "Pony has helped me to take control."

"I'm sorry that happened to you. Was it here in Saskatchewan?" Wouldn't it be something for Pony to rape a woman and then pull her into his stable to *help* her?

She shook her head. "Out west." She pushed her hair back from her face. It looked damp as if she had come from the shower.

"I need to talk to you about last Saturday. Do you remember what you did?"

"Sure. I was on chicken duty. I cleaned out the coop then scrubbed down the water jugs and refilled them."

"I meant more like in the evening."

Chapter 52

MY HAND HIT MY DESK as I walked past it for the fourth time. "All three of them admitted to going to the Greek Saturday night with Pony. I thought I was going to have to push on one of them, but they were all more than willing to say he was there." That wasn't sitting right with me. I just can't be happy. Paige watched me as I paced around the desks. "Smug little prick with his pretty hair thought he could lie to me and get away with it. The video doesn't lie. His own patients or followers, or whatever you want to call them, even said it was his idea to go there."

"Sounds perfect."

"Yeah, sure I can place Pony at the bar, but now I can't place the victim at the bar so the point is mute. His lawyer was right. If I can't place the two of them together then I don't really have a crime."

"Have you wondered if Pony is even your guy?" Paige played with the bandage wrapping her hand.

I stopped my pacing. Of course I had thought about if he wasn't the killer. That's all I could think about. "Pony lied about where he was Saturday night. He was there and I have proof. Why would he do that? I mean, he did look genuinely surprised when I showed him that he was at the Greek Saturday night though." My brain drifted back to River's interview.

"The asshole just left us there," River blasted out during her interview. "He left the bar and took off with the car, so the three of us had to get a ride with somebody else."

"What car was he driving?"

Her eyes looked up at me with that Millennial scorn. "The. Car. I don't know cars. The silver one that we don't have anymore."

"The one that was stolen three weeks before this incident?"

Her arms wrapped around her body as she turned with a sigh. "I don't know."

"Who gave you the ride home? Was it Sheriff?"

She turned back to me and blinked a few times. "Who?"

They all gave three versions of the same thing. Did that mean they were all telling the truth or that they had all been coached? Maybe they were part of it. Maybe they did it. The only story that was different was Pony's. I thought everyone loved him. Didn't he save all of their lives? If they were coached wouldn't they be trying to make me think he had nothing to do with this? I had to find out who these people were. I had to find out who Jane Doe was.

"What's next?"

I dropped into my chair. "I'm going to talk to the bouncer at the Greek. I have to do background checks on, I don't know, everyone. I have to find a new avenue to get me to," a sigh escaped me, "wherever it is I'm going."

"Steel," Bisson was pulling his coat on as he stopped at my desk. "Have you talked to Vista about your problem?"

First thought, lie. Second thought, he already knows the answer. "Not yet. I will call him and deal with it right now."

"Good. Are you okay to go home?"

"I will be, yes." Liar. All day I had been noticing people looking at me and whispering just out of my hearing. It was getting under my skin, however, I preferred that to going home. In headquarters nobody would actually say anything to my face, except for Delaney. At home, in my neighborhood, I was already hit by one person. By now Cheryl had probably told everyone about the pictures and they were ready to brand me. Maybe she even kept some to show everyone that lived around me. Assumptions were going to take over. I had to go home sometime though.

Chapter 53

WHEN I GOT TO THE GREEK Brew Pub the real busy action was still a couple of hours from starting. They wouldn't have a bouncer at the door until 8:00pm when people began to go out.

Before I left HQ I called Vista and asked him to meet me.

It wasn't going to be an official police report, but I was going to talk to him about it. I followed Bisson's orders...technically.

I looked to Pony's corner before taking a table by the brewing equipment. They weren't there. While I waited I took out my phone and used social media to look up the Stable members I had interviewed.

There was a lot from and about River. Jordann Avery, as her profiles called her, had been on just about every site before she went to the farm and since then all of her pages sat in limbo. She had been popular at one point with lots of likes and comments on every photo. Then her posts slowed down until completely stopping.

Dove, Heather Turtle, only had Facebook and Instagram, as far as I could find. Nothing had been posted on either since joining the Stable. She had pictures of her playing sports and enjoying life with friends. There was nothing showing any family.

As for Wylie Teller, Coyote, there was absolutely nothing. No Facebook, Instagram or YouTube pages. There was nothing on Twitter. He had no social footprint whatsoever that I could find. In this day and age that almost made him not exist.

I looked around the room and didn't see anyone looking back at me. It was nice to not have everyone looking in my direction or whispering as I walked down the hallway. Nobody in here knew I was a degenerate.

I did a quick search online for my pictures. Faryn Steel naked. Nude female cop. Faryn Steel, threesome. I couldn't find a thing, so I sent a text to Brandi's husband. As a novelist he was excellent at finding things online. I finished it with telling him to get Brandi to give me a call. She had been at the scene of a vehicle collision most of the day, too busy to respond to my texts. It was nice being in a room of people that haven't seen me fucking, but I still wanted to know where those pictures were.

As soon as the waitress came I ordered an ice water with lime, got the food menu and asked if Antony could come over when he had a chance. It wasn't until I sat down that I remembered the only thing I had eaten since toast at Brandi's was ice cubes.

"If you order anything but the pork ribs this meeting is over." Greg Vista let his weight drop into the chair across from me. "You look like shit. You're much better in the pictures."

"Don't even go there." I fingered my hair out. It had been a long day and I needed to relax. "Where did you see them?"

"I haven't." He turned to the waitress appeared with my water. "I'll have a Coors and Greek ribs. Extra Greeky."

"I'll get the ribs too, please. You haven't seen the pictures? Someone said they were online."

"Maybe, but I haven't seen them. All I know is from what you told me and what I've heard about."

"Heard? The city cops know about them? Oh my God."

"Relax, Faryn. It's out there. I'd like to see them myself. Purely for the fact that I need to know what I'm talking about, of course."

I took the 4x6's out of the bag with my tablet in it, checked that nobody was around and slipped them across the table like face down playing cards. As he flipped them over his eyes told everything. I would have loved to have been sitting across a Texas Hold'em table from him. "These ones were thrown at me this morning by my neighbor. She also gave me a right hook." The puffiness had gone down but the colours of a bruise were coming out behind the cuts.

"You pressing charges?" He quickly put the pictures down as the waitress brought his beer.

I shook my head. "I don't care about the punch. If anything I can understand it. I just want to find out who is trying to ruin my life. Taking the pictures, leaving them around, giving them to the neighbor kid, emailing them to work colleagues." My phone rang. I saw Jimmy's name and sent it to messages. "Sorry. That guy might be someone to check out. My ex. If I didn't have a badge I'd beat him down myself."

"I'll start with the neighbor with the right hook first. Nothing came up as far as instances in your neighborhood. Does anyone have a grudge against you?"

Every time the door opened I expected to see Pony and the gang.

Didn't River say something about pictures even before they were everywhere? She would have had to find out where I lived and somehow be there on that night outside my window. They were right over in that corner when I had a drink with Emery and Grady and I wasn't paying attention afterwards. Someone could have followed us from the Greek. Followed. I thought a Volkswagen Beetle followed me from the Stable. Why would River want to screw with my life? How did she email everyone?

"Faryn, you still with me?"

I turned back. "Yeah, sorry Greg. Someone in the case I'm working right now might have it out for me, but I don't want to put them in there yet."

"I'll talk to the neighbor and her boy and see if I can find security cameras around Studio Fitness and go from there."

"Hey guys," Antony the bartender walked up to our table carrying two plates. "Greek ribs, extra Greeky? And regular Greek ribs for you, Corporal."

"Can you sit?"

The bartender looked around for a moment. The crowd was steadily growing, but, things were still in control. "I can sit for a little. How can I help you?"

I didn't bother introducing Vista. "You dated Marta St. John, right?"

"Sure. Long time ago."

"I've been looking into her assault. Is there anything you can tell me about it?"

His eyebrows went up as he shook his head. "No. We weren't really talking by then. I gave a statement to the police after it happened. Why the interest?"

"The case I'm working on might be connected. I'm just seeing if anyone remembers anything."

"Like I said, I wasn't talking to her for a while before it happened and I was here working that night."

"Okay. You said on the phone that the bouncer from Saturday works tonight."

"Yeah," Antony got to his feet. His muscles bulged making his shirt look two sizes to small. "He should be here soon. I'll send him over before he starts. Enjoy your meal."

Vista was already halfway through his ribs. He had some of the bones cleaned and didn't care about what was going on around him. I followed suit and dove into my plate of pork ribs slow roasted in Greek seasonings and lemon juice, lemon roast potatoes and vegetables. There was tzatziki sauce on the side. The succulent meat fell right off the bone. It was so good to put fuel in me and my body was happy to take it in. I was almost done when a big man joined our table.

Chapter 54

"I'M CORPORAL FARYN Steel, what's your name?"

"Jeremy." He was tall with a broad chest and muscular everything. He wasn't over abundant with muscles, but you could tell he could handle himself. His blond hair was shaved short, probably to stop anyone from grabbing it. There was a bruise under one eye. Occupational hazard. Other than that he had a pleasant face.

"Have a seat. You were working the door last Saturday night, right?"

"Eight to close."

I cleaned my fingers on a paper napkin. "I wonder if you remember seeing someone." I saw Vista eyeing my last two ribs and pushed the plate toward him.

Jeremy snorted. "I usually don't remember anyone unless I have to toss them or choke them out. Then I just remember them to make sure they don't come back."

"This one you didn't let in. She was wearing a brown dress. She was with a group of women that did get in."

"That could be anyone. I don't let a lot of people in and they all come in groups."

I slipped my tablet out and took a moment to set up the surveillance video. "This is from here Saturday night. I'll show you the group that supposedly left their friend outside."

"Oh the college girls," that took a couple of seconds.

"The college girls?"

"Faryn," Vista put his hand on my shoulder. "I have to get going. I'll let you know about that other thing."

"Thank you. Let me know if you get anything."

"I don't know if they're college or university girls, but they're in here every weekend," Jeremy said as soon as Vista was gone. "They should be here soon." He twisted around to search the room.

I felt my heart race. This was it. I was going to find out who this woman was. Like I haven't thought that before. "Do you know any of their names?"

"First names, yeah. That's Kate, she used to be a server here. She quit to go to college fulltime. That one is Chelsea and, ah shit, I don't remember the others' names. I'm sure Kate introduced them to me, but unless I choked them out," he finished that sentence with a shrug of his shoulders.

I had one hand under the table in a tight fist. The nails dug into my palm trying to calm myself. "Do you remember the one you didn't let in?"

"Nancy? Maybe. She forgot her ID at home, I guess. I knew who she was and that she was of age, but policy says no ID, no entry. She didn't have it. I said no way and she told the others to go in without her."

Nancy. This could be her. The amount of people in the room was building. They only used a bouncer on busy nights to help keep crowds down and keep the trouble makers at a minimum. Antony looked at our table every time the door opened. I understood what he wanted, but this guy knew my Jane Doe.

"So Nancy, did you see where she went after you wouldn't let her in?" Please tell me Pony came out and got her into a silver Dodge Neon.

"No, I was busy. I didn't really notice. I think I remember her talking to a woman with brown hair, but didn't see who." He pushed himself halfway up from the chair. "I really have to get to work. If you stick around I'll signal you if the college girls get here."

After he left I settled back in my chair. It had been a really early morning and a long day on top of that. My eye lids were burning. I just wanted to go home and sleep. That wasn't happening. Jane Doe could be Nancy. I wasn't leaving until I either talked to the people she had been with or herself, if she wasn't my victim. This seemed too good to be true. Or was this going to be another dead end?

Chapter 55

FRIDAY NIGHT AT A POPULAR bar was not the place I wanted to be. Even with the music, growing crowd and loud murmur of conversations I caught my head bobbing as I drifted off.

I stuck with my ice water and gave the waitress a polite smile every time she looked at my table for four with just me at it sipping free water. I was taking up space and not spending money. I was just about to give up and leave when I saw Jeremy wave at me and point to the side of the room. A group of young women collected at a table near the entry to a small room with slot machines.

I took a gulp of water, got up and made my way toward them. I glanced in Pony's corner. Still not there.

Maybe he wasn't on the prowl tonight?

There were five women around the table and two men. All were in their twenties, most dressed in casual attire. One woman was wearing a tiny little skirt below a low cut blouse and another had a sheer blouse and painted on jeans. Not the smartest choices in cold weather. I was just as stupid almost twenty years ago and wasn't much smarter now.

"Excuse me," I had to raise my voice to be heard, "I'm Corporal Steel. I need to talk to some of you."

They all stared at me. The moment I showed my credentials I got a couple of, "oh shits," in return.

"What did you do? One of the girls shoved one of the guys. She had black hair perfectly teased and wore a lot more make-up than she needed. She was the one in the black skirt which barely hid anything.

"Nobody has done anything," I said. "I need to ask you some questions about last Saturday night."

A few of them looked at each other. They were all trying to telepathically talk to each other about what they did last weekend.

"Who do you want to ask?" This was from one of the guys. Casually dressed, baseball cap holding down a mop of hair, good-looking enough. I knew a few guys like him in high school.

I looked at the paused image on my tablet. "I think you four ladies. Chelsea, is it?" Short skirt looked surprised that I knew her name. "Kate?" Short blue and green hair dressed in a plaid top and jeans. "And you two. I don't have your names yet."

"Michelle." Long blond hair, big doe eyes wearing leather pants and jacket.

Sheer blouse crossed her arms over her chest. "I don't have to tell you my name." Her eyes were glassy.

"Stop being a bitch, Tara," mop hair smiled behind his beer. "Oops."

"Why don't the four of you come outside with me so we can talk without yelling?"

"But it's cold outside."

"I'll make it as fast as I can." I waited until all of them were up and walking toward the door. Tara moaned something about bullshit.

"So you were all here Saturday night? You had a fifth with you when you got to the door though." They looked at me and then each other with blank expressions. The four of them stood close to each other, all hugging themselves to stay warm. I would like to say they all put on sensible jackets before stepping outside, but I couldn't. "She couldn't get in."

"You mean Nance?" Michelle was already sucking on an e-cigarette.

Tara snickered. "Stupid bitch forgot her ID."

"It could happen to anyone." Chelsea pulled the lower hem of her skirt down. It bounced back up.

"We were here for her, Chels. It was stupid to go out for her and then she forgets her ID. Really, who does that?"

"Have any of you heard from Nancy since Saturday?"

They all shook their heads.

"That was the point, wasn't it?" The coat Tara had put on before going outside wasn't much more protection from the cold than her top. "She quit school and was going away. She wanted to work on cruise ships or yachts or something. We weren't supposed to see her anymore."

"Why did she quit?"

Chelsea stomped her feet to keep warm. The heels probably weren't doing it. "She said she couldn't handle school life. It was taking her to a bad place and she couldn't keep up. Her words."

"And you can?" That sort of slipped out.

"I have a 4.0 GPA, I'll have you know." Chelsea's lip went into this bitch face snarl. I knew people like her in high school too.

"Sorry, I didn't mean anything. What is Nancy's last name?"

"Harrelson."

"Address?"

"3231 Tulloch Avenue. Apartment 3C, but she was supposed to leave Sunday morning for wherever she was going. Did something happen to Nance? Why are you asking questions about her?"

"Shit," Tara stared right at me. She seemed to forget about the cold. "This is about that, that news report isn't it? The girl in the brown dress you're looking for."

Saw the report and didn't put it together that it was her acquaintance. Interesting. If Nancy Harrelson was Jane Doe I was going to have to look at everyone she knew. These, friends, were questionable. I thought avoiding their questions for the moment would be a good thing. "Any idea what she did after she couldn't get in?"

"She said she would wait in the car, so I gave her my keys." Kate was the only one with a respectable winter coat. "About thirty minutes later she texted me saying she was going to leave, so I met her outside again and got my keys back."

"Did she say where she was going? Did you see her go with anyone?" I wanted to ring the answers out of them. They were already buzzed before they got to the Greek. Buzzed enough that it took a while to get anything out of them. Their twenty-something minds didn't see the danger women were in every day. They didn't get what they had done. "Well?"

"I don't know. We were having a good time and I just went back inside."

They were having a good time, so they left their friend alone to the animals. They could have changed plans and gone somewhere else, returned to her place for her identification, anything. They just left her.

Chapter 56

THE AIR WAS CRISP AND the wind came from behind me blowing toward the Greek doors...I smelled him before I knew he was there.

"Excuse me," he said.

I flinched. Goosebumps were on my flesh inside my coat and not from the cold.

Pony nodded as he slipped past me, gently grazing my elbow, walking between the young women. River, Coyote and Dove followed behind. River was laughing as she moved around me. Coyote looked up at me for just a second. The corners of his mouth twitched up before he dropped his gaze and shuffled on. It was a if he hesitated, wanting to say something, but couldn't bring himself to do it. I could see how people flocked to them. They were cool, aloof. The walking Zen.

"That guy gives me the creeps," Kate stared at the door to the pub.

"You know him?" Someone outside the Stable who could actually say something about Pony. And thought he was creepy and not the savior of the afflicted.

Kate nodded. "He used to work here."

This was new. No one I had spoken to has said that Pony had worked at the Greek. Antony didn't say a thing about it. This was how he hunted. "When was this?"

"A long time ago. I don't remember when. I just remember the way he looked at people."

"Did you work with Marta St. John? She worked here a year and a half ago." She said she met Pony at the Stable. Why would he be working at the bar, besides having his prey right in front of him.

"Oh yeah, I liked her."

"Can we go in? It's cold."

I shot Tara a look that shut her up. "Did Pony work with her?"

Kate looked at the others then back at me. "Who? I meant Wylie. He washed dishes here for years before he stopped coming to work. No call or anything, if I remember right."

Wylie, not Pony. My breath seemed to fizzle out. That could have been how he was sucked into Pony's world. Maybe Pony talked to him or he heard someone talking about it. A place that claimed to fix your wrongs and help you center yourself could be a strong enticement. Something I had to find out about.

I wanted to stop and think about Pony for a moment, but I had to stay focused. "Does Nancy have a boyfriend?"

"Don't think so."

"Are we done here or what?" Tara's voice went to a whine. "It's fucking cold."

I took a breath. "Give me your names, phone numbers and addresses. I'm sure I'll be talking to you again."

Chelsea and Kate didn't move as the others went inside. Kate was the first to speak. "Why are you asking about Nance? Is she...was she that woman you found?"

"The body," Chelsea added.

My head nodded and shook at the same time. My hair bobbed around. "It's possible. I'll keep you informed."

I had a name. That was far more than what I had this morning.

Chapter 57

"NANCY HARRELSON SAID the apartment was going to be vacant as of when?" Her apartment building was secure. Anyone could get into a lobby with mailboxes and food delivery menus, but needed a key or to be buzzed in to get through another door and into the building.

"This past Monday." Doug was the live-in building manager. I had to ring his buzzer twice before he answered on the intercom. As soon as I told him who I was he came to the front door. "But she's paid to the end of the month, like I said. I told her I wouldn't start showing it for at least a week in case she wanted to take her time getting things out."

"That was nice of you. Have you cleaned it?"

"No. I haven't had the time. I haven't even gone in the room yet to check it out for damage and shit." He pulled a ring of keys off a magnetic clip on his belt. He had a fresh tomato sauce stain on his shirt and smelled of body odor and garlic. He flipped through the keys until finding the master and unlocked 3C. There were dried flowers hanging above the peep hole in the door. "Do you need me to stick around?"

I knocked on the door as I opened it slightly. There was a cardboard box just inside over flowing with shoes. All the lights were off. "Hello? Police." To Doug I said, "I'll let you know when I'm done."

I called into the room again. The refrigerator was humming. Warm air blew from the furnace vents. No reply was returned. Under most circumstances I would have needed a warrant to step foot in the apartment. In this case the renter told the building representative that the room would be vacant five days ago, therefore I just needed his consent. I flicked a light switch and the energy efficient bulb in the ceiling flickered before getting bright.

As I stepped inside I took a pair of blue rubber gloves from my pocket and tugged them on. Every time I did that I thought of a silly quote from an old TV show. "Two by two, hands of blue." Shiny.

Inside the front door was a closet, nothing inside it, then a small hallway with openings to other rooms. There were small nails in the walls with nothing hanging from them. I squatted to check the box of shoes. Slippers, flats...nothing expensive.

The first room on the left was the living room. Small couch, empty bookshelf, flat screen television in its box leaning on an empty stand, game system in a box, boxes of books, painted masks wrapped in newspapers and framed photos in cardboard boxes. All of the boxes were piled by the entryway ready to be carted away. Again, there was nothing on the walls but nails, hooks and outlined shapes of things made by dust.

The kitchen was across the hall. Cupboard doors were open with nothing inside because everything was in boxes on the counter top. There was nothing on the refrigerator door and inside was a couple bottles of water, two apples, a small carton of milk and an open box of baking soda. This, for sure, was the apartment of someone ready to leave. All she needed was a truck and she was ready to go.

The bathroom was not as organized. There was make-up around the sink, a hairbrush inside it, a yellow towel had been discarded on the floor next to the tub and bottles of shampoo, conditioner and body wash sitting on the edge. The towel was dry. There were no water droplets in the tub or on the walls or shower curtain.

I put the toothbrush and hairbrush into plastic bags to match DNA.

The bedroom had a stack of four boxes and a couple of large suitcases by the door. There was nothing in the dresser or closet. The bed coverings were scattered as if someone woke and tossed them aside. It definitely didn't seem like someone had been here recently.

There was a cup of Tim Hortons coffee on the bedside table. A shake told me there was a little still inside. One close sniff said it was moldy. As I was putting it back I saw what had been underneath. A brochure. The title was what stopped me. Welcome to...The Stable.

"I got you, you son of a bitch." My earthy voice echoed in the empty apartment.

This was my connection to Pony. I still couldn't place him directly with Nancy on Saturday night, but I had her knowing about him. Maybe he couldn't wait for her to be right in front of him. He saw his chance to pounce and went for it.

There didn't appear to be a crime that took place here, so I didn't need the crime scene techs to tooth and comb the place. I went into the boxes trying to discover who Nancy Harrelson was and why she was making all of these life changes. I found photographs in one box. She was pretty with long brown hair, like Jane Doe, a pointed chin and pleasant look about her. A photo album showed she had been to Paris, Greece, New York. She liked to ride horses. I moved on to other boxes and the suitcases to see she had some fancy clothes, but nothing too extravagant. She wasn't living above her means. Her shoes were all knockoff brands. She was an average woman with average things living an average life. My kind of gal.

It was almost eleven when I walked into my house. I still had my gun, so I locked it in my lockbox in the bedroom. We weren't supposed to take it home, but if we did it had to be locked up just like anyone else.

I poured a glass of Captain Morgan and sat at my small dining table with my laptop open.

For the second time today I was using the modern police's strongest tool...social media and the way people were so open with their lives. Nancy was twenty-two and from the east coast. She had been in the nursing course at the University of Saskatchewan. From what I could tell she didn't have any family. Most importantly, nothing had been posted on any site since last Friday. "Almost done packing. New life starts Monday." Fifty-six likes and twelve people asking what she was going to be doing. Not one reply.

Nancy Harrelson was my Jane Doe. Just that thought made me relax. I knew who she was and I knew she was involved with Pony somehow. The moment I knew that I felt sleep creeping up on me. In the morning the investigation was going to begin again.

DAY SEVEN
SATURDAY

Chapter 58

THE DIGITAL DISPLAY on my phone read 2:25am. My doorbell was ringing. A knock followed.

Was it them again? I held my breath as I stared into the darkness of my room. Someone could be waiting in the black shadows of my house for me to go answer the door. One hid somewhere, bathroom maybe, as the other knocked to get me to come out. As I stumbled down the hallway...my mouth opened and I took a breath.

I thought about my weapon locked away in its case. My skin tingled. I could take it out. I could also accidentally kill someone needing help.

I held my breath and listened. It was as quiet as Nancy Harrelson's place. The heater was blowing. The fridge was quiet at that moment. I could hear an engine humming though. In my driveway?

A light moved around. A flashlight was being pointed through a window. How many times had I done that when looking for someone?

A fist pounded on the front door. Four bangs.

Something else was moving. A coloured light.

I swung my legs out and pulled on a pair of sweatpants and a hoodie. I left the key for my lock box on the bedside table. Every light switch got turned on as I walked past them until my house was almost glowing. I glanced at the baseball bat just inside the door before I looked outside and saw a uniform.

"Faryn Steel?" Two uniformed police officers stood outside my front door. City police. One pointed his flashlight through the window as the other spoke.

"Corporal Faryn Steel, yes. Do you know what time it is?" Freezing air blasted through the door. The temperature had severely dropped since the sun went down.

"Yes ma'am." He introduced himself and his partner. "Is anyone else in the house?"

Did they expect others? Did they see the pictures? Were they expecting an orgy? "No. Can I see your credentials?"

They both showed me their badges and ID. He continued, "what were you doing this evening?"

"Are you serious?" He just stared at me. "Okay, around 7:00pm I had dinner at the Greek Brew Pub with Sergeant Greg Vista, you might know him. Then I talked to some witnesses at the pub and went to a suspected victims apartment. I got home by 11:00pm and have been here ever since." I bit my lip before asking if they wanted me to describe my bathroom habits before bed. "Do you want to tell me what this is about?"

"Could you step outside please?"

I took a step back. Under Canadian law police officers who did not have a Feeney Warrant couldn't step into a house to arrest someone. They had to have them come to the door and hopefully step outside where they didn't need that specific warrant. A suspect could wave at you from inside their home and there was nothing you could do about it until you had that paper in your hand. These men looked like they were going to take me. "What's going on guys? Give me some professional courtesy and tell me what's happening."

"Someone was attacked outside a country bar earlier tonight."

"Was it Jimmy?"

I saw the cop's eyebrows raise. "We need you to come in for questioning."

"Is Jimmy okay?"

"Please come with us."

"Is he okay?" I slipped into my black ZeroXposur jacket keeping the fur lined good down.

He put his hand out like he was asking me to dance. "You'll have to talk to the investigator."

Chapter 59

"HOW. THE FUCK. IS Jimmy? I had been left in an interview room for over an hour until a constable and a sergeant in the city police criminal unit joined me.

"We'll get to that, Faryn." Sergeant Malcolm Reynolds took the seat across from me. It was the same type of room I had Pony and the others in. "Why don't we talk about what you were doing earlier in the evening."

"Call Vista. You call Sergeant Greg Vista right now." I didn't like being a suspect. I didn't like knowing what this felt like. I was pissed off and nervous and worried about what I was going to say, even though I knew I didn't do what they were accusing me of. The longer I sat there the more I began to think I actually might have done something. I wondered if I had ever had someone in the box and they admitted to something just to make it all stop.

"We did call him. He should be here soon. Greg isn't really a morning person." Reynolds was trying to be friendly.

"The morning is the best time of day," I made a face.

"Not for him. Can you tell me about Jimmy?" Nice little jump there in the topic department. He was good at this.

I let out a sigh. I was better. "Can I get a cup of coffee?" I was tired and cranky and I wanted to give Vista some time to get his ass in there. I tugged my coat in. It was warm, but I didn't feel comfortable.

"Here's your coffee," Reynolds slid a paper cup across the table after five minutes of watching me look for split ends before stepping out to make it. "Jimmy?"

"He's an ex boyfriend. I hadn't seen him for a while, but I knew he was in town and then he stopped by work the other day to say hi. What happened to him?"

Vista slipped into the room making enough noise for the other man to notice him. He leaned himself against a side wall.

Reynolds obviously didn't like having him in the room. He lost his edge. "At 11:30pm last night he was leaving the bar where he had performed the last few nights. He was struck from behind and fell to the ground. When he looked up there was a group of people around him who proceeded to kick and punch him. The attack resulted in several cracked ribs, internal bleeding, lacerations, a fractured cheekbone and a popped eardrum. They also broke several fingers on one hand. He'll recover, but it'll take time."

"And why did you bring Faryn in?" Vista's morning voice was more of a low growl. He tried fingering sleep gunk from the corner of his eye.

Reynolds turned to him. "Jimmy reported that one of his attackers said, Faryn Steel says to leave her the fuck alone." He fixed his gaze on me. "I hear that's the vocabulary you like to use."

I flipped him the bird. "Do you really think I would get someone to beat him up?" My head tilted. I couldn't help myself. My smartass mouth got me in more trouble than I could remember.

"You did tell me you would beat him down if you didn't have a badge." Vista's whole body shook when he giggled.

"I said, I would beat him. What kind of person do you guys think I am? He posted a YouTube video of me and keeps calling and texting all the time, so I was mad at him. He came to my work and embarrassed me in front of coworkers. In front of a suspect! I'm annoyed with him and I'm pissed, but I'm not going to screw up my life over this guy. I even gave Vista his name as a possible for harassing me over the last couple days. Am I really going to give you his name and then send people after him? People who would use my name openly like that? I'm being set up."

"You think this is connected to the harassment?" Vista sipped coffee from a takeout cup. Nice of him to stop on his way in to helping me.

"What harassment are we talking about?" Reynolds looked from one to the other. I nodded to let Vista inform him about what had been going on.

"Where's Jimmy now," I asked as soon as he was done. "I want to talk to him."

"That's not happening. As far as he is concerned you were responsible for his attack. He's recovering."

"And I wasn't." I was tired of being accused. I was supposed to be the good guy. "How many people attacked him?"

"Four. The one that spoke was female." Reynolds was giving me too much information. He knew I wasn't guilty.

I rapped my knuckles on the table and leaned back on the chair as much as it would allow. "Right there you know it's not me. I would have got bikers to do it. Big, scary ex cons that know to keep their damn mouths shut."

"You're not helping," Vista said. "Any witnesses?"

Reynolds shook his head. "Not a one. The guy is lucky to be alive, you know. I mean, they didn't have to stop hitting him. They just suddenly stopped and left. It took over ten minutes before he was found."

"Of course they stopped. They're trying to ruin my life, not put me in prison for the rest of it."

"You really think this is connected to the harassment?" Vista dropped his cup in a garbage.

I collected my now auburn hair over my shoulders. "You have a better reason for it?"

"Besides you wanting to give your boyfriend a beat down? Nope. I would say random violence, but the use of your name doesn't match up." Reynolds stroked his chin.

I flattened my hands on the tabletop. "And if you actually thought I did it you'd be charging me." I pushed myself up and walked around the table.

"Where do you think you're going?"

"To get a good coffee." I gave them a wave with my fingers as I left the room.

Chapter 60

"FARYN!" CHERYL LEAPT from her lawn and charged across the street. "I saw the police pick you up. Serves you right! You should be ashamed." It was like she had been waiting for me to get home. The taxi dropped me off at the curb and there she was on her curb waiting to spit venom. Even Chow-Chow barked at me from beside her feet. Did she really have nothing better to do at 6am on a Saturday morning? "Do you hear me?"

I ignored her and headed for my house. She said something else against my character and got a single finger in the air as I walked away.

It was pointless to say anything. It would get us into a shouting match on the front lawns of the quiet suburban street and with my luck she'd be left to spy on everyone and I'd be picked up for disturbing the peace.

Someone was out to get me and Cheryl was at the top of my list of suspects. She was enjoying this too much. It was probably the best gossip she had found out in years.

I honestly didn't think she was vindictive enough to do any of it. Especially not beat up Jimmy who was number two on the list. The secret photographer, possibly, but I doubt he would put himself in the hospital just to screw up my life. Emery and Grady could have had the pictures taken, but it would have been for their own fun. A naughty boost to what we were doing. There was no motive for them to do any of the rest. The pictures Emery found at the gym could just as easily have messed her life up. River didn't like me so I could put her on the list, but how would she have access to where

247

I lived or worked out? How would she know about Jimmy? Could she have convinced a group to beat him up? Not likely. Wendell across the street might have taken the pictures and could have passed them around so all of the high school boys could stroke one off, but there was no reason for the personal attacks or for Jimmy. And then, of course, I had to put Pony on the list. Maybe he didn't like my suspicions?

The next question was, who had I put in jail that could do all of this?

I unlocked and opened my front door. My foot kicked something. Where was the change from the cold outside to the furnace warmed house? Where was the heat? There were engine sounds. They were still loud even after I shut the door. I shouldn't hear anything.

I flipped the lights on. My collection of shoes were scattered across the floor. Jackets had been torn out of the front closet and strewn all over.

"What the fuck?"

There was a noise in the dark of the house. Someone was there. My hand went to my hip and grabbed my sweat pants. My gun was at the back of the house in a drawer in my dresser locked. I reached for the baseball bat. It wasn't there. Damn.

I stared through the kitchen toward the dark hallway. I had to get to the knife set in the kitchen.

The fridge and kitchen cupboard doors were all wide open. A jar of pickles had been smashed on the floor. It looked like every piece of food had been thrown all over. The photo albums from the table had been opened and pages torn out. My pictures were in the mess. The All Valley one was melting into a spill of milk. Something cracked beneath my shoe. The Captain looked up at me from underneath. Son of a bitch.

Something shuffled ahead of me.

I reached for the small flashlight still by the microwave. I swept the light toward the hallway. Clothes were spread all over. Nothing moved. My hand swept to the living room.

Red eyes stared at me. A dark shape twisted and leapt through a hole in the living room bay window. Dog? Coyote? Demon?

Glass was of the floor and furniture. The back-up propane tank from my barbecue was now on my living room floor sitting on top of the flat screen.

I stormed out the front door and sprinted down my driveway. "Are you fucking serious?"

Cheryl turned. She had her hand on her doorknob.

"You're up in the middle of the night and see me getting picked up by the cops, but you don't notice someone breaking into my house and trashing it? What the fuck? Selective much?"

"I wasn't up to see you get arrested." Cheryl's fingers fought with the doorknob. The dog in one arm struggled. She wouldn't stop staring at me.

I stopped suddenly on her lawn. My body tilted forward before correcting itself. Everything was shaking. I forced my fists to open. I was in enough trouble already. "Then how did you know I got picked up?"

Chow-Chow dropped from her arm. It yelped the moment it hit the ground and ran under a chair. "We have a security camera. Chow-Chow, come."

"Answer me!"

Her body froze. "The camera has motion sensors. I, I saw that it had taped something when I got up, so I sped through the video and saw it. I stopped watching the video then. I didn't see anyone else. You stay back."

I took a step toward her. "You have a camera on my house?"

"What? No." The door popped and opened slightly. "It's pointed at the street. I can see a bit of your yard, but that's it. Chow-Chow, come."

I took another step. Cheryl pushed her little dog through the doorway with her foot, followed and slammed it shut. I head the deadbolt click.

I glanced up and saw two security cameras on the corners of the house. One was pointed at their front door and the other right at where I stood. They blended into the house enough that somebody messing with my place might not have noticed them.

Chapter 61

"YOU HAVE TO TALK TO Cheryl about her security cameras. How many days footage does she have? Maybe you can find out who's been to my house. Maybe it's caught on her security videos." I bounced on my heels next to my truck. The cold was biting through my coat. The sweatpants did very little for keeping the cold from my legs. I wished I was at least wearing underwear.

"I will," Vista said. He showed up by himself and insisted we stay outside until the crime scene unit arrived. "Have you gone through the house yet?"

"Just quickly. They took my lockbox with my service pistol in it. Probably have the key too." I stared across the street at Cheryl's house. The curtains kept moving.

The sergeant waited until I noticed he was quiet and turned back to him. "Don't you think you should have started with that? Jesus, Faryn." The crime scene unit van pulled up in front of Vista's car. "Where was the box?"

"In my thong drawer."

"You have an entire drawer for thongs?"

"Yes."

He nodded as he wrote everything on a pad.

"Get the security video from her for the past week and I'll bet you'll see who's been doing this."

"They broke your bay window on the other side of the house. What makes you think it's the same people?"

I raised my arms. I didn't know why this was happening. All I knew was that I wanted it to stop. "I'll bet you the people that took those pictures also beat Jimmy up and broke into my house. They were waiting for the cops to pick me up. They planned everything."

"What if they were just waiting for you to be asleep? Maybe us picking you up last night was a happy coincidence that stopped you from being raped and killed?"

I hadn't thought about that or I didn't want to. I could have been the next person with something shoved up my orifices. I started with shaking my head and then my entire body shivered. "I grew up being an independent woman. Not the victim of anything. If they wanted a piece of me I'd take some of them out."

"Speaking of victims, I looked into that thing you asked for," Vista lit a cigarette. "Counting Naomi Fuller, we've had three cases in the city where shoes were reported taken. A man got attacked jogging along the river. His attacker beat the crap out of him with a pipe and then took his wallet and sneakers. Then there was a lady that was jumped. Her clothes were torn off, paint was dumped on her. Luckily for her someone came along and scared the attackers away. They took her shoes with them though. And these are just my cases. I emailed you the files."

Investigations were all about patterns. It was deciphering them that was the hard part.

Chapter 62

I USUALLY HAD WEEKENDS off, but not while I was deep in a case. I left Vista and his people at my house and headed into headquarters. Another neighbor said he had boards he would put up over the window and secure my house as soon as the police said he could. At least somebody didn't think I was a slut. But then maybe he saw the pictures and had hopes like Delaney. As long as the window got boarded up. Something else to deal with later.

I changed from the sweatpants to black leggings and a black tank top from my workout bag. It wasn't exactly professional but was better than sweats.

Step one at the office was look further into who Nancy Harrelson was. No criminal record. Her parents were deceased. She did appear to have a sister that lived on the east coast. The only way to know if it was Nancy was a DNA match. I had dropped the hairbrush and toothbrush off to Ident before going home last night. Now to hurry up and wait.

I looked through the files Vista sent me. None of his cases were as violent as the rapes and murder. Were they even connected? Maybe it was a coincidence, though, how many criminals out there would take shoes?

Maybe I should have checked my own shoes to see if any were missing before calling the Vista this morning. I didn't have many shoes to begin with, so it wouldn't have been hard to check.

I wanted to think about something other than what was happening to me, but my mind continued to drift back.

It seemed like Nancy had no one thinking about her. Her friends, acquaintances was a better word, were more worried about their next drink last night than why I was asking them about a friend. They went to the Greek all the time. Kate had worked there. She said Coyote had worked there as well and that she knew Marta St. John. Coyote might have known Marta. Maybe there was more to the shy guy that what I had seen? I had pieces to the puzzle, but none of them were connecting.

I picked up the phone and dialed. "Hi, Marta, good morning. It's Corporal Steel. I'm fine, thanks. How are you? I'm sorry to bother you, but I wanted to ask if you remember a guy who worked at the Greek when you did. His name is Wylie Teller. He would have been a dishwasher. No, just checking on things. Thank you." She didn't remember the name, so maybe they weren't there at the same time. I hung up and went back to the computer.

Nancy's friends were on every social media site with varying security features, mostly minimal. They posted about their lives and shared just about everything anyone else posted. The one thing none of them seemed to have was anything about Nancy. I found a picture of her on Chelsea's Facebook. A group was rafting and there she was squished in with everyone else smiling and holding up a can of beer. She was the hang along friend. The one that was in the group, but not really. She was always added in as an afterthought.

"Are you hiding?"

I knew that voice and didn't have to look up. "You never called me last night."

"It was a long day," Brandi said. "Huge car accident, multiple vehicles, multiple victims, no straight stories. Anyway, The Man said to tell you he couldn't find your pictures online anywhere. If they are online then they're hidden well and not out there for everyone to find."

"And if anyone can find a naked woman online..."

"It's my man!" She pulled a chair close. She used her fingers to toss her short hair. The amber had multilayered of color. "Anyone bugging you about the pictures?"

"Delaney had some comments, but mostly I get looks and hear whispers. I'd rather have them say something to my face. At least then I can fight back and see who the assholes are."

"The world needs assholes. Where else would the shit come out of?"

I couldn't disagree with her.

"How's your face?" She got in close for an inspection. "That bruise came out."

"I've been hit worse."

"Have you heard from your friends?"

I shook my head. I tried texting Emery and Grady yesterday and again this morning but was getting nothing back from either.

Brandi leaned back a little and interlaced her fingers. "Rumor has it you had a rough night."

I rubbed my eyes. "I'm tired of rumors and people talking about me."

"In other crappy news, none of the fingerprints from Pony, River, Dove or Coyote matched the print from the shotgun stock."

"Of course not." I crossed my arms on the desk and put my head down. My hair draped down on the sides of my face. Three hours sleep, always looking over my shoulder...I was running out of steam.

"Come on." Brandi got to her feet. "Let's go. Road trip."

I absently stood up, slipped my feet back in my boots and followed her toward the door. My brain was being eaten by the Millennials Facebook posts that I had been reading all morning. A collection of quizzes and food photographs that didn't mean a thing. "Where are we going?"

"Wakaw detachment called. We have to go see some twins about an eyeball. You can tell me about yesterday along the way."

"Sure. Wait, what?"

Chapter 63

TELLING EVERYTHING that happened on Friday took almost the entire trip to the Thompson-Bing house near the murder scene. Talking it out just emphasized what I didn't know. What happened to Nancy outside the Greek? What do the Stable members know? Who was out to get me? Why? Where was my gun?

"Is that all they took?"

One of our police vehicles was in the driveway as we turned in. The constable got out and stepped around his truck.

"I'm not really sure," I said as I stepped from the Ident SUV. The cold hit me and I zipped up my coat. It seemed the temperature was getting lower. "As soon as I saw my gun was gone I called it in, so I didn't have time to look." I nodded at the constable who tried to hide a smile as soon as he recognized me. His gaze didn't stay on my face.

"Shoot her!" One of the blond boys ran across the driveway between us. It was one of the boys that found the body of Nancy Harrelson.

His twin chased him. "Shoot the zombie!"

"Corporal, no shadow today?" The constable was another one not shaving his moustache.

"My what?"

"Constable Garrett. I thought she was shadowing you. I've had to fill in her shift."

"She's looking into something for this case." I had sent Paige to do secondary face to face interviews with Nancy Harrelson's friends. They weren't criminally negligent, just inconsiderate assholes. Other than her text saying, ok, I hadn't talked to her much since the day before.

"The call said something about an eyeball." Brandi had her gear in hand and was ready to work.

"I'll let Mr. Thompson tell you about it. I surrender the scene to you."

A man walked to us from the house. He wore thick pants, filthy jacket, wool toque and was pulling on leather gloves. He smiled when he got close and deep dimples sunk into his cheeks and matched one in his chin. "You're the detectives?"

"Corporal Faryn Steel. This is Constable Brandi Faye, the crime scene tech."

"Like on TV? Like CSI?" One of the boys was suddenly beside us. Was it Andy or Zeke?

His dad waved his hand. "Go do whatever you're doing."

"Hunting zombies."

"Go!" He ran off after his brother. "Times change, eh? When I was their age we were pretending to be soldiers. Now it's zombie hunters. Probably their damn video games. I only let them play them for so long and then they have to go get into their own trouble. Sorry, my name is Garth Thompson."

"You were at the game last Sunday when I came here. How was that?" My hands were stuffed in my pockets. Leggings were no better than the sweats had been.

He shrugged. Most Saskatchewan football fans were serious about their devotion to the Roughriders. They wore their green and white proud, even during the losing years. "We lost. Have to wait for next year, I guess. Come on, I'll show you what I found.

"I was taking firewood from the pile and putting it in the splitter. I picked up one piece from the top and saw something. I got closer and realized the damn thing was staring at me. Scared the shit out of me, to be honest. I covered it up and went in the house to call the Wakaw detachment."

We followed him to a pile of log pieces cut big enough to fit in a fireplace just like the ones Pony and his group had been cutting. There was a tarp on it, so snow had gathered over it. On one side there was a three-sided building with cut and split logs already stacked neatly inside. A machine between the two. It was used to split the cut logs in half.

"It's under here." He lifted a blue tarp.

Brandi jumped forward. "I'll get that." She put gloves on and carefully lifted the tarp. "Yeah, it's an eyeball." She leaned in close. "There's marks on it like from a bird, maybe. I would guess a crow took it from the body and dropped it as it was flying. I've seen it before."

"Is it Nancy Harrelson's?"

"I'll have to send the eye in for testing to see if it's hers, but I'm guessing it is. Unless someone else is missing an eye."

"Are you talking about that lady from Sunday that the boys found?"

"Yes, you left early that morning, right?" I opened my notebook. "About what time did you leave?"

"I went outside at 4am. Sarah was going back to sleep after getting me going and the boys were still sleeping, so I didn't want the guys waking them. The boys get into trouble if they get up early. I knew my buddies would blare their horn if I wasn't outside, so I made sure I was out there early. Work has been crazy and I haven't done anything for myself in a long time. This was my one thing. Me and the kids haven't even gone hunting this season. We usually go a few times."

"Did you hear anything that morning? See anything?"

He nodded. "I walked over here to wait for the guys because I can see right down the driveway and when I looked at the field I thought I saw something moving." I nodded for him to continue. "The moon was still out, so it was pretty bright. I had my binoculars for the game, so I used them to take a look. I thought maybe it would be a deer or moose, but then I saw it had two legs. I thought I saw, like, what do you call it? A ponytail. And there was like, reflective stuff on their legs too. Like on hers." He pointed at the silver reflective lines on Brandi's tactical pants.

We both looked at each other. "How long was the person out there?"

"I don't know. My ride came and I left. I thought maybe it was a hunter getting their spot before the sun came up. Lots of geese in the fields. Do you think that was the killer? Am I going to be in danger for telling you?"

"No sir." I closed my notebook and put the pen back in my pocket. "There's no reason for you to worry about that. You've been a big help."

"I'm good here, Faryn." Brandi had the eyeball in a container and had photographs of everything.

Everything changed with that eye.

Chapter 64

"ARE YOU THINKING WHAT I'm thinking?" Brandi didn't even have her seatbelt on yet.

"Probably not." I closed the passenger door. My phone chimed in my pocket. "I don't know what I'm thinking."

Brandi put the SUV in gear and got us going toward Wakaw. "I didn't mention this to you, but did you notice Paige's email address wasn't in the email with the pictures of you? I tried mentioning it that morning but we all got busy. I looked over everyone it was sent to and even had The Man look at it. Her name was not there. Now, she might have been out at the body before it was called in."

"Whoa, slow down. Mr. Thompson said it was someone with a ponytail and reflective striping on their pants. That could be anyone. Sure doesn't mean it was a cop. It sure doesn't mean it was Paige. I don't think she would rape someone, beat the snot out of her and then go back for a double tap. Nancy had semen in her. You have an answer for that?"

"She and Pony are a team. Okay, maybe she's not the killer, when you say it out loud like that, but what about the personal attacks? She could still have done those. Does she know where you workout? Does she know the layout of your house or about Jimmy?"

"She might, but then so do you." My phone chimed again.

"So now you're accusing me of trying to ruin your life?"

"I never said that." Battles were fought on what people thought they heard. I took my phone out and used my thumb to bring it to life.

"I like your life, Faryn. Your life is my entertainment."

"Then you owe me the price of a ticket." I read the texts on my phone. "Drop me off at the Wakaw detachment."

"Why? How will you get back to the city?"

"Paige will give me a ride. She says we need to go see something at the Stable, so she's going to pick me up."

Brandi looked at me longer than she should have before looking back to the road. "You sure that's safe? Paige could be the one messing with your life."

"Brandi, stop it. I just met the woman a week ago. What reason would she have for messing up my life? What reason would she have for killing Nancy Harrelson?" I said the words, but thought about how she had been upset the morning I met her outside the Thompson-Bing house. She said it was her relationship. She hadn't really talked about the man she had been seeing since she was in the emergency room. People didn't always want to talk about their lives. That didn't mean anything.

Chapter 65

"SORRY YOU HAD TO WAIT," Paige smiled at me from the driver seat of her personal car.

I didn't pay attention to the four door sedan as I slipped into the passenger seat. My mind was more on how she reacted to me. "The other constables kept me company."

"Shit, did they tell you stories about me?" There were lines in her cheeks when she smiled.

Yes. I answered with, "no. They mostly told me about their own glory days." In reality they said Paige was a good officer. She could be distant and had a short fuse, but otherwise good instincts. She kept to herself a lot and they didn't know much of anything about her personal life. It wasn't easy to get things out of them without making it look like I was asking. "So, what's going on at the Stable?"

"That guy, Coyote, he called HQ looking for you. I was there, so I took the call." Her foot pushed down on the gas pedal as we exited the slow zone on the highway. "He wanted to tell you he found something and it was really important that you get out there to see it. I knew you were out this way, so thought I'd come get you."

"He happen to say what it was?"

"No. He sounded really nervous though. He said we had to get there before they came back."

"Maybe he found some evidence against Pony." I wasn't sure what to think about everything going on this morning. All of it was spinning around inside my brain. Having just a couple hours of sleep wasn't helping me focus on any one thing. In my head I saw Pony's pretty face and messy hair and I heard Brandi saying he and Paige were a team, Katy saying Coyote creeped her out, River talking about the pictures. Nothing was what it seemed. "Can I ask you again about Sunday morning when the body was found? What time did you get to the scene?"

Paige glanced in my direction. "Okay, I was already in my truck, so I got to the Thompson-Bing home about 8:20 in the morning. I questioned the mom and the boys and then I walked to the field to ensure there was a body and called it in. I went back to wait at the witness residence after the next unit arrived at the scene."

I pulled down the visor to pretend like I was checking myself out and not seriously interviewing her. I wished I had the time to take care of my hair. The auburn strands had that messy, fresh from the shower look. "That was the first time you saw the body?" And my eyebrows needed some attention. Paige's sculpted ones that showed every emotion were annoying.

"What?" She looked at me and one of those brows was arched up over an eye with perfectly applied mascara. Bitch. "Of course. Why are you asking?"

"Inconsistencies on witness statements," I said. "How was your night last night?"

She snorted. "I heard you had some night."

"Who did you hear that from?"

"One of the guys from city police. It must have been crazy, eh." Paige stared ahead at the highway.

"Seriously, who told you?" If I went with Brandi's theory Paige was probably sitting in the bushes at 2:30 watching as the police lead me to their car so she could go throw my propane tank through my window.

I saw her look in the mirrors. Did she not want to look at me? "I honestly don't remember, so many asked me if I knew what happened. That and the pictures. I keep getting asked about those. I told them to mind their own business. Oh, Coyote said he found a hidden box. That's what it was."

"A box? That's a bit vague."

"He seemed really excited."

"I thought you said he sounded nervous?" I tried not to be obvious about watching her. She wasn't a bad guy. Or I wasn't seeing it. Did the sweat on her temple mean anything? Did the lack of her looking at me mean she was guilty? Did Brandi make me paranoid?

As we turned onto the Stable driveway I saw the yellow Volkswagen and pick-up were gone. It was Saturday, so there was the farmers' market in the city. Compared to the other times I had been here this looked like a ghost town. The only person around was the young man that jogged out from the barn as we left the car. Wet glistened off his shaved hair. Coyote wore a green camouflage jacket that looked too big for him. A lit cigarette twitched between his lips.

"C-c-c-c," we waited until he got the words out, "c-c-c-Corporal, you came."

"I was told you had something to show us."

He nodded and spun around. Without a word he started walking toward the barn. I glanced at the house then the fire circle. It certainly seemed like there was nobody else there.

"Where's Pony?" My stomach twisted. Paige walked beside me and a step back. This wasn't right. We shouldn't have been there. My fingers grazed my thigh where my pistol should have been.

"He's not here."

"Where is he though?"

"G-g-gone. He and s-s-s-s-some of the others left." Coyote turned slightly to talk over his shoulder.

"Where's everyone else?" As if on cue the house door opened and the man who had been doing firewood with Pony, Dove and Coyote the other day stepped out. He waved before lighting a cigarette, but never left from the front of the house.

There were footprints in the snow in all directions and worn paths going to the animals and the barn. It made the fact that nobody was moving around all the more obvious.

I glanced to the gardens to see the plants still there were dusted in snow. The tomato plants had been pulled. Everything was now in limbo until spring.

I looked at Paige. Her hands were in her pockets. Her expression said she wasn't worried, so why was I?

She gave me a nod and said, "where are we going?"

Coyote sidestepped again as he looked back. A long tube of ash disintegrated from his cigarette where it had been desperately holding on. His ears were red from the cold. "To the b-b-b-bb-bbb-BARN." A growl escaped his throat. "S-s-sorry."

"Your stutter is really bad today. Something bothering you?" The more we got to the center of the property the easier it was for the wind to get to us. I fought the urge to put my hood up.

Coyote smiled. "N-n-nervous, I guess."

"Nervous about us or nervous about Pony?"

"It's in here." He pulled a metal bar back to unlock the barn and walked backward pulling the large door with him. Some light came through the windows, but it was still dark the deeper inside you looked.

At the back was a tractor that even from the door I could tell it was something recycled from some farmers field. There were obvious dents along the tire wells that were splashed with rust. Inside the door to one side was a box made of wood pallets. Inside that were an assortment of garden tools – hoes, rakes, shovels, what have you – all waiting for next year. Behind it was an old washer and dryer which had seen better days. A couple of push lawn mowers were along one wall. What sort of therapy was it to have to cut all their grass by push mower? Scrap lumber pieces had been pilled above our heads on the exposed rafters. The back half had a set of stairs going to a loft above. There was straw piled back beside the tractor, old windows leaned on the wall behind them. I got the scent of oil and dirt the moment I stepped in the open doorway.

"Where did you say Pony was?" I half expected this to be some thriller movie and I would see his scruffy hair step out from behind something at any moment.

"He left. It's right there. What I f-found." I followed Coyote's pointed finger to a cardboard box sitting in front of the tractor. It had the company name, Tanimura & Antle on the side with Romaine written underneath. It was originally made to hold twenty heads of lettuce, so it was a fair size.

"What's in the box, Coyote."

He looked at it and then to me. "P-Pony and the others left, s-s-so I looked around to help you. I wanted to help you."

"What's in the box?"

He stared at me for a long second before blinking and going on. "I-I-I l-looked around t-trying to find ... I-I didn't know what I was looking for, but I knew P-p-p-p-PONY! spent a lot of time out here alone. Then I found this."

"What's in the box?"

Paige snickered behind me. "What? That was very, Brad Pitt in the movie Seven." She stared at me. "You know. That part when he gets delivered the box and he's like, 'what's in the box,' and it's a head."

"I know the movie." I shook my head, but, to be honest, the corner of my mouth did curl up. Nobody was moving. I stepped forward and still the others didn't move. The wind blew making the barn windows rattle. I knelt down and quickly opened the top flap of the box. I wasn't expecting what I saw.

At least it wasn't what it was in the movie.

They were shoes. Women's heels and pumps. I pulled my phone from my pocket and snapped a couple of quick pictures. Sitting on top were a pair of black heels. I recognized the glue mark where one 4 inch heel had been stuck back on. These were my "fuck me" heels.

Chapter 66

"WHAT ARE YOU DOING with these?" When did I last see my shoes? Weeks maybe. How did they end up here? "What are you doing with these?"

"It's not me." He seemed to shake.

"What are you doing with these?" I repeated. I knelt down in front of the box.

"I found the whole box back behind there." He pointed to the right corner. "I didn't even know what it was at first. Is it important?" Coyote leaned over my shoulder. His hot breath touched my ear.

I barely wore heels, so I couldn't remember the last time I wore the black ones in the box. They were the ones I wore out to parties or dates when I wanted to feel sexy. These did everything right as far as making my legs appear longer and my glutes tighter. Working out did a fine job, but every woman could use help.

I took a rubber glove from my pocket and tried to move some of the shoes slightly without actually shifting their position. They were not all women's shoes. Beneath a pair of blue pumps was a man's dress shoe. Underneath mine were blue and white sneakers, size eleven. That could be Vista's case of the guy jogging along the river. These could all be shoes from people that were attacked. Trophies. I counted nine pairs. On the side, one on top of the other was a pair of block heels and beside those were open toed strapped shoes with a spike heel. Naomi Fuller and Marta St. John.

A black heel underneath mine had a shiny surface. I picked one of mine up, careful to barely touch it, and moved it over. The one under had a platform toe. That shoe could be anyone's. Even the red sole underneath marking it as a Christian Louboutin didn't mean anything except that it was expensive. Or did it mean more?

I moved some others quickly and found the pair. It had a dark smear of crimson along the toe. They could belong to anyone.

I knew them. I had seen a pair of those very same shoes on my kitchen floor a few days ago. I took them off Emery myself. These couldn't be hers. She never said anything about being attacked before and she just had them days ago. It was against my training, but I touched the smear. Brandi would yell at me for that. It streaked. It was half wet. These were new to the collection. The blood was new. They went after her.

Emery.

My eyes flicked up. Coyote had moved and was crouched down across the box watching me. His blue eyes stared at me, watching what I was doing.

"What the hell is this?" My heart raced. My mind went through everything this could mean. Emery. "Where did you find these?"

Coyote straightened up. He seemed to grow in height. "I found the box back – back there." He pointed off to the left near the stairs going to the loft.

"These shoes. Where did these shoes specifically come from? There's blood on these. See this? This is blood." I waited until he looked where I was pointing. He blinked a lot then looked at me with wide eyes. "Where's Pony?"

Coyote's mouth dropped open. His eyes twitched.

I looked the way his eyes had gone. "What's up those stairs?" Every word that came out of my mouth came twice as fast as I intended. There wasn't time for this.

Coyote hesitated. "It's the loft. Pony won't let anyone up there."

"What's up there?"

He shook his head. "Um, um Pony doesn't let anyone go up there. That, that's his sanctuary."

I looked up the stairs as if something was going to come down. I turned back to the young man. "Is Pony up there? Is he?"

"He left," Coyote stared back at me. His hand rubbed a cheek with very faint fuzz on it.

"You stay here." Without another word I walked toward the steps.

"Faryn, do you want-"

I turned enough to point at the man in the green coat. "Paige, you keep him down here."

At the top was a closed door. I glance back at the man to see he was standing by the box of shoes watching me. His mouth was slightly open and tongue barely poking out. I turned back to the door. Maybe he was lying to me and the rapist was right on the other side of that door. My fingers flexed at my right side. If something came out of that door I was going to be stuck. I should be calling for back up. I should back down the stairs, get back to the car and call for other officers to come. Instead I took another step up and reached for the door handle.

It turned and with a slight push the door opened. I held my breath. I heard my breathing and the wind making the barn boards rattle. Nobody jumped out at me. Waiting?

"Corporal?" My heart jumped. "You want me up there?"

I couldn't see either of them from the top of the stairs. "No. Stay down there."

The room was lit by sunlight through windows. The walls were dark with a lot of things attached to them. They were small squares. Probably 4x6 size. I stepped inside, my eyes darted around.

There were no other rooms and nothing anyone could hide behind. It was an open square room. There was a table on the far side with a printer sitting on top.

The closest wall had pictures, the same size and glossy surface as the ones that were left on my doorstep. I shouldn't step inside. I needed to call back up. I walked to the wall and looked at the photographs. They were of people, men and women. There was blood in some of them. Faces looked twisted in pain and some had clothes torn off. One picture had a woman tied to a bed, her face eyes to the side, mascara smeared on her cheek. It was Marta St. John.

It was his victims. There was a man wearing shorts, the jogger. A woman was face down on the ground. I couldn't see her face, but it must have been Naomi Fuller. I looked at another. I didn't want to find either of them. Someone crying. Blood coming from an eye. A woman frozen in a scream. Victim after victim. I didn't want to see her. I didn't want to see him. I didn't want to see any of them anymore. Three pictures were stuck side by side like a comic strip. A woman's face – pretty, her face as it was hit with something that was blurred, her face after with a large open gash on one cheek. Anger. Hatred. It was all right there. Pony had collected these as he did the shoes.

I got to the end of the display and there I was. The pictures of me having sex with Emery and Grady. Most were stuck to the wall with tacks. One had hunting knife through the picture and two centimeters into the wall behind it. The blade was pierced through my bare chest.

The printer on the table had a stack of photo paper beside it and cords coming out. The ends could be plugged into a phone. His own personal photo booth.

This was his place. This was where he planned and waited and built himself up before destroying a life. This was where he celebrated after.

I turned to go back. Eyes stared at me. I stepped back and my hip hit the table and I saw another person who also stepped back. Her eyes looked crazed. No. That was me. There was a full length mirror beside the doorway and I was looking at myself. My hair, mahogany dyed with red highlights, was on my shoulders. My face looked different. My eyes were crazy. That reflection wasn't me. It was a woman out of control.

"Where is he Coyote? Where's Pony?" I charged toward him the moment I got downstairs. I stopped and looked down at the shoes. It was hard to tell if all the pictures were of different people or if some were the same person. It all seemed more than the amount of shoes were in the lettuce box.

This was wrong. Pony wouldn't have left them sitting around. These were a serial rapists, *a killers*, trophies to excite him when he couldn't be on the hunt. He would have had them hidden in the loft where nobody would just stumble on them, but he could return to them. They should have at least been upstairs with the door locked, not in a cardboard box in the corner. And a pair of shoes with still moist blood should not have been there.

They couldn't be Emery's.

"Where the hell did he go?" I glared at Coyote. His eyes looked so large I felt I could have seen my own brown eyes reflected in them.

"Faryn," a hand grabbed my shoulder. I spun away and raised my fists. "Jesus! What's going on? What was up there? What does this mean?"

I blinked and came back. Coyote wasn't my suspect. He wasn't the source of everything. I focused on Paige and her worried expression. "You see these black shoes? These are mine. The only way someone could have got them is if they had broken into my place last night. These shoes here...Emery has a pair of these. This looks like blood. Pony couldn't get to me, so he went after her."

"What? No. Those shoes could be anyone's."

"They're a twelve hundred dollar pair of shoes, Paige. How many women in Saskatchewan would have these?" Emery may not have wanted to talk to me, but I still cared about her. I didn't want a relationship with a single person, however I still had strong feelings toward the people I was with. I knew those were her shoes.

Paige put her hands up. "Let's calm down. You don't know that. You call your friend and make sure they're not hers. I'll step outside and call Ident and get someone to come process the shoes and whatever else you found." Paige headed outside to make her call.

I already had my phone in my hand.

I glared at Coyote, though he didn't seem to notice. He stared down at the box of shoes with glassy eyes. He reached a hand up and rubbed the side of his neck. The Omega tattoo disappeared behind his fingers.

The phone rang and rang against my ear. Nobody was answering. That didn't mean Emery was in trouble. She could have been in the shower. She could have been tied to a chair with Pony ready to skewer her.

Nancy Harrelson's shoes. Marta St. John's shoes. Naomi Fuller, the jogger, my shoes, Emery's shoes all wrapped up in a romaine lettuce box and handed to me in the center of a barn. It was too simple. Pony left them there to get me going.

"Faryn,"

My skin goose bumped instantly. My hand went to my bare hip. After a moment I realized I was holding my breath. Jumpy.

Coyote stared at me with his blue eyes, "I might know where Pony is."

Chapter 67

"WAKAW IS SENDING SOMEONE to babysit the box until Ident can get here. What did you find upstairs?" Paige spun on the ball of her foot as we walked past her at the barn door. "Where are we going?"

"For a drive. Coyote thinks he knows where Pony is." I slipped my cell phone into my pocket.

"Should we call a unit?" Paige had to quicken her pace to keep up with me.

"He doesn't know the address, just where to turn. We'll see where it is and call whenever we know that he's there."

Paige looked back at Coyote who rushed to keep pace. "How sure are you?"

"Pretty sure. He said he was going to see his special friend and he took me there once. I can get us there."

"Faryn, are you sure he even knows where he's taking us? If this is a wild goose chase we'll look like idiots. And taking a civilian along is ......-"

"It's on me, Paige. If we get in trouble it's all my fault. You drive. Coyote, back seat."

My main thought was, were Emery and Grady alive? If that was either of their blood on the shoe then I was responsible for every moment of pain they went through. Pony liked to use foreign objects in his victims. Emery could be somewhere screaming. Nancy Harrelson was the only one I knew of who had been killed so far. Maybe there were others. Maybe he liked that feeling.

And what about Grady? He would have put up a fight that could have got him killed. Maybe that was his blood on the shoe. Pony found them. Grady fought. His blood splashed on Emery's shoe. It was possible. It was easy.

"Turn left."

Paige signaled before putting the car on the highway in the direction of Wakaw. I glanced over my shoulder. Coyote grinned and nodded.

It was all nice and easy. Pony did everything. Pony hurt all of these people. He took the pictures outside my house. He harassed me. Easy.

Last night he was at the Greek. Later he beat up Jimmy. Then he broke into my home, trashed it and stole my weapon and my shoes. He drove all the way out to the Stable and put my shoes right on top of all the others in a lettuce box. And Emery's underneath. Why would he do that?

He took shoes as trophies. Maybe it started with taking them to stop his victims from getting help, but then he got off on it. He collected their shoes to relive the events. He wouldn't leave them where someone would stumble upon them. Or would he? Maybe that was the excitement.

Marta St. John was attacked in her home. Why take her shoes?

I looked at Coyote. It was too easy.

A group attacked Jimmy. There was a lot that had to happen in one night. The attack, the break in...when did he go after Emery? And then he went back home, put shoes in a box and left again?

My mind spun. It was all there but wouldn't fit just right. In my interview with Pony he swore he wasn't at the Greek Saturday night, but in the security video he was. How could he not know he was there? Was it a bluff? I heard Dove's voice in my head. What did she say about her past?

The turn signal flashed.

"Turn right up here," Coyote said.

I looked at Paige. Pony said something at his interview. He named someone. I turned in my chair to see Coyote. It was only then I realized I hadn't put a seatbelt on. "Who is Sheriff?"

His eyebrow went up. His lip twitched. "Who?"

"Pony talked about Sheriff. I'm assuming that's his Stable name. Who is he really?"

Coyote stared at me. I didn't like being under his gaze. "Sheriff who? Sheriff Dillon?" His mouth turned into a slight smile. He held me with his eyes. Nancy's friend said he creeped her out and I could see that. His eyes popped wide. "Sheriff Rosco P. Coltrain. Coo, coo, coo!"

My breath caught. The Omega tattoo on his neck was almost pulsing. "Who is she?"

"Oh it's a she now?" His smile grew. "Maybe it's Sheriff Pat Garrett chasing after Billy the Kid down in New Mexico." His eyebrows bounced and eyes twitched to the left side. Both his hands went up with finger guns raised. "Pew! Pew!" Coyote's mouth opened and he laughed.

I looked at Constable Paige Garrett behind the steering wheel. She stared at the road ahead. Coincidence. Why did she pick my up in her personal car? She was supposed to be interviewing Nancy Harrelson's friends. She should have picked up an unmarked car and gone out, so how was she at HQ to get Coyote's call?

I turned back to see Coyote staring at me. He nibbled on his lip. His eyes looked excited. Was there really a call?

"You seem to have lost your stutter, Wylie Coyote."

"I had one a most of my life and now I don't. Didn't you know I'm the Stable's picture of success in all its glory. Come in troubled and then leave, well, whatever I am now. I guess Pony really is to blame for everything, isn't he? He let me see my potential."

"And what is that?"

"Confidence in myself. Confidence to lead others. The world is full of people looking for someone to lead them, Faryn. Sometimes sitting around a camp fire talking it all out doesn't fucking work. Sometimes you can't get rid of the anger you feel by talking about it. Sometimes all you need is a family who understands. Sometimes you need to own your anger." He took a breath. "I do say, Faryn, you look like the mouse who just figured out that getting the cheese is really a trap."

I looked at Paige. "You put the turn signal on before he said to turn."

She glanced in my direction but wouldn't let her eyes meet mine. They flipped up to the rearview. "This guy's nuts. You're letting him manipulate you."

"Somebody has been manipulating me, for sure."

Coyote made noises in the back seat. It wasn't laughter, but joyous sounds. A toddler bouncing and cooing with excitement. I didn't want to look back and see him staring at me. Did this make him the killer? He had something to do with it and he was taking us away from everything. He was enjoying this.

"Paige, pull over," I said. Out of the windows there was nothing but white. Fields and frozen sloughs together made a snowy landscape. There were not many homes on the highway we were on. I knew a farm with a house on moorings was coming up. After that there wasn't much for kilometers. We were going somewhere that I didn't want to be. "Pull over."

She shook her head. Her foot never left the gas pedal. "I can't. We have to keep going. We have to find Pony and save your friend. Isn't that what we're doing?"

"I said, pull over."

A tear ran down her cheek. "I can't."

Coyote started humming.

"Constable Garrett! I gave you an order."

Paige stared straight ahead. "I prefer, Sheriff."

There it was. I reached for the keys.

"Now," Coyote yelled.

I turned to him.

I saw the back of Paige's fist.

My head pushed into the headrest before I even heard the snap and felt the pain. My eyes watered instantly. Blood exploded from each nostril. The world spun.

Chapter 68

"IT DIDN'T HAVE TO BE this way, Faryn." The car had stopped. Paige was leaning in front of me enough that I could smell her hair.

I felt steel on my wrists and the distinct sound of handcuffs tightening in front of me. As Paige moved back to the driver's seat I tried focusing on my hands. Red lines snaked across everything I looked at and moved. It took a second to realize it was the veins in my own eyeballs. My hands didn't look right. They were all red and vibrated.

"You caused this, Faryn."

"Fuck you." I spat out a clot that splattered on my knee. "You're really crossing this line, eh?"

Paige put her nose close to mine. "We are Omega. We made the line and you pushed me across."

I looked at my hands trying to find a spot I could run under my dripping nose. I settled on a clean spot on my forearm, smearing bloody snot into it. Pain surged across my face. My nose was broken for sure. I tasted my blood in my throat and felt my face starting to swell. My neighbor had nothing on Paige.

The car started rolling again. It was then I realized Coyote was quiet. There was no more humming or giddy noises from the back seat.

I forced my eyes opened wide. I had to see. I had to focus. The outer edges of my vision were still out of focus. "You guys sound like a cult."

There was a groan from the back seat. "I knew you'd say that." Coyote kicked the back of my seat. "Try to be original, *Corporal*. What is a cult? Do you know, Faryn? Do you know the definition of what a cult is?"

I spat again. This made the man in the back seat snort.

"The definition of a cult, is a group with a strong belief and devotion towards a person or object."

I didn't bother turning around. My eyes felt like they were being pulled in all directions by little fish hooks and taut line. "Do you guys have a belief or you just go around brutalizing people?"

"Do you know what the biggest cult in history was, is?" Coyote ignored my question. "Come on Faryn, you had so much to say before."

I spit a gob on the dashboard this time and side eyed the driver. She changed her grip on the steering wheel, but acted like she didn't notice. Playing sports with boys when I was young made me tough and able to spit. "I did before your traitor pet sucker punched me."

Paige didn't say a thing. The back of her right hand had my blood on it.

"Just answer my question." He sounded bored and in my mind I saw his eyes roll. "P-p-please, Faryn." Coyote faked a stutter and giggled.

"I don't know." I raised both hands and wiped my lips. "Jim Jones and the People's Temple? Scientology? I don't fucking know, alright."

Coyote laughed. "So far off." He kicked the back of my seat again. "It's Christianity."

"That's a religion not a cult."

"Is it? It's a group of people with a strong belief. The second part is a devotion towards a person or object. Billions of people have a cross in their homes or around their necks. They have bibles and pictures of their white washed thought if Jesus. Do you know the difference between a cult and a religion?" He used the back of my seat to pull himself forward so his mouth was near my ear. "Time. Christianity was a cult when it started. Time passed, people joined and it became a religion."

I turned my head slowly and stared into his blue eyes which were staring right back. I wanted to head-butt the son of a bitch. "So you're starting a religion? What the fuck is Omega?"

I knew where we were on the highway. Soon the scenery was going to change from fields and sloughs to forest and fences. I had an idea of where we were going too.

Why didn't I see it before? Ten kilometers down the highway the road would make a left turn and slope downward to a green bridge over the Northern Saskatchewan River. The highway went up a hill on the other side. The car wasn't going up the hill. It would turn right on a road just across the bridge. A kilometer down there was a large three story house with an attached two car garage. Cream walls, chestnut trim, new window treatments every six months, groomed professionally taken care of lawn in the summer, Jacuzzi in the back. Grady's house.

"The end of everything," Coyote said. "That's what Omega is. The end of hiding and doing what's expected."

"Where does the raping and killing come in?" The hit had cleared my mind. I had to think about where we were going and what I was going to do. I didn't know what would be going on whenever we got where we were going. All I knew was that there was no help coming for me. Human sacrifice came to mind.

"Raping and killing," his voice took on a mocking whine, "raping and killing. *Raping and killing.* The woman who screws indiscriminately shouldn't judge. How many orgies have you been a part of? Maybe you should ask our so called victims about their innocence. And for the record, we never killed anyone."

"Nancy Harrelson? Why kill her? You've never killed before."

"The anger went too far, so something had to be done, but I didn't kill her."

I looked at Paige. She stared at the road ahead. Her skin looked grey and moist. Some of my blood spatter left little spots of red on her chin. Pursed lips tightened even more. "What about you, Paige? You don't want to answer that question? What about the pictures of me? Was that you or River?"

"Me," her voice was barely a whisper.

"Seriously? Brandi's never going to let this go. She knew you had something to do with it. Or should I even worry about what's going to happen after today?" The left turn before the bridge was coming. After the turn there was a house just before the river with a covered horse riding arena and a few sheds. As far as I knew it had been abandoned for years. "Is the plan to kill me?"

I was looking at Paige, but Coyote answered. "We haven't thought that far ahead yet. I'm sure Paige would be happy to do it again."

She flinched. She glanced at Coyote in the mirror.

"How did you really hurt your hand that night I met you at the hospital? I'm assuming there was no married man or a window."

"I did punch a window. I had to do something to make you come running."

"So torturing me was, what, a good time? I should have known that tattoo on the back of your neck wasn't a lucky horseshoe." A tear ran down Paige's cheek. Her fingers tightened on the steering wheel. I was getting her worked up. People made mistakes when they got worked up. "You're crying now? You're a cop. You're supposed to stand for something. You broke my fucking nose. You killed a woman."

Paige opened her mouth then closed it without a word.

"We had to distract you somehow." I heard Coyote smiling as he spoke.

"But I didn't suspect you of any of this. I didn't suspect any of you. It's been Pony the whole time."

Coyote pulled himself forward again until his nose was close to my ear. I turned to look at him and for a moment I thought he was going to kiss me. I smelled the cigarette on his breath. "You ever think, maybe that's the problem? We lead you down a path toward the great Pony, but maybe we changed our minds and we wanted the glory for what we went through. What's life without some gratification? The girl to acknowledge your existence, the guy to give you the attention he gives someone else, the superior who just isn't what they think they are or the person who did you wrong. And maybe there's even someone else who has that career you won't have. The anger builds and builds and something has to be done. They're the alphas in the world, but we are the omegas. They don't see us. They begin everything and we end it. A to z."

"How many others have you raped and killed? Did you use the pipe on the girl or did Sheriff?" I looked at Paige. "I'm guessing you beat Jimmy." I hoped the doors of the car were like in my Dodge.

Coyote clapped his hands making a show of it. "So righteous. You are no better than us. You have primal sexual urges and you let go. You give into them. The most pure emotions any human has are anger and jealousy. There's no faking those. We feel. We react. The anger builds and when we can't take it anymore we release."

"What made you react to Nancy Harrelson?"

"She was a pretty young thing," Paige said blankly.

"And what happened to her?"

Coyote raised his hands. "You have to ask River. She did most of the dirty work."

I looked ahead of us. The corner was coming. What I was thinking was stupid even without handcuffs. If the door didn't unlock with a pull on the handle I was done.

"She was pretty," Paige said with a breath, "and she was there. River wanted to have her fun, so I picked her up. She did most of the rest, mmm, with some help from Pony."

"How is Pony involved."

"I can't tell you everything." She braked for the corner. The back end of the car started to swerve on the ice. She straightened the car and braked again.

I grabbed the door handle and pushed.

Chapter 69

MY HIP HIT THE GROUND first. The skin tore on my lower back. My Shoulder hit next sending pain erupting through my skull. My legs were thrown as I rolled and the world spun around me.

My body tumbled and rolled into the snowy ditch before stopping. I was sure I wasn't moving anymore, but everything felt like it was still in motion. The handcuffs dug into my wrists. Rocks were embedded in my skin. I didn't want to move. I had to take an assessment of myself first.

I heard the car break.

I forced myself up with my forearms. Every muscle and bone screamed. No, that was me. I couldn't think about the pain in my head or my back feeling like it was on fire. I wanted to lay down on the frozen ground, curl up and wait for Coyote and Paige to get to me.

My legs pushed up.

My knees hit the snow. My face was next. I felt the cold. Snow. I felt wet on the side of my head. Blood. Burning in my back. Pain. I had to move.

I pushed up again. The car whined in reverse. Run Faryn!

My knees wobbled. Everything in front of me was out of focus. Everything slid side to side. Run!

Ahead was the house with boarded up windows and doors. I saw three houses. I had to get to the buildings before turning to the river. They were my only cover.

I forced my legs to work as I broke into a run. Paige had her gun on her. They could have my gun. I felt bile shoot up my esophagus, turned my head and let it go. My feet stumbled. My hands touched the ground. I pushed up and kept running.

"Shoot her."

My feet had to move faster. If they were going to start shooting I had to be behind something like the buildings. Once I got to the river I was out in the open the entire way, so it was delaying the inevitable.

"Get her then!"

Fuck it!

I turned toward the river. I had to get across it. Finding cover would just give them more of a chance to catch up. I just had to run. I had to get to Emery and Grady.

"Faryn, stop. I'll shoot."

Thin willows had grown to take over the old houses yard. They slapped at my skin as I plowed through.

The river. At this point it was about a football fields length across. I didn't see water. There were places along the river where it was still open. There was a hill and trees on the other side. Cover.

I broke from the willows and skidded down a small drop. I ran onto the ice without hesitation.

When the water was flowing it moved fast at this part and it was likely moving fast beneath the surface. Ice chunks had crashed into each other starting at the bridge pilings creating points of ice sticking up like icebergs making an iceberg parking lot. It was like a snowy mountain range.

Cracks echoed in the air the moment I stepped on the ice. Something glistening caught my eye farther to the right away from the bridge. Water. It was on the far end of the ice chunks.

"Faryn, stop!" Closer.

I hurdled over an ice chunk as high as my knee.

As I stepped on another the ice bobbed down. Water bubbled up around it. My balance changed. I landed on one knee and pushed up quickly.

"Faryn!" Paige grabbed my shoulder.

I spun as hard as I could, my hands clasped together. I saw Paige's eyes go wide. My knuckles hit her chin with a satisfying crack. Her head snapped to the side and she stumbled.

My foot arched in a crescent kick in front of her. My foot was right on target. The heel of my boot hit her hand sending her service pistol into the air.

Paige dove at me spearing her shoulder against my side. Her arms wrapped around me.

I braced myself to stop from falling. Ice cold water splashed over my boot. I brought my elbow down on the back of her neck with all the power I could muster. Bone meeting bone felt exhilarating. Again. As it hit the back of her shoulders a third time her hands dropped. I spun. This time my clasped hands connected square across her cheek with a crack.

She stepped back.

Her foot hit a chunk of ice and her body pitched. Icy water sprayed into the air. The chunks separated. Paige's arms and legs flailed splashing more water.

"Help!" All her other words were lost as the frozen water punched the air from Paige's lungs.

Cracks spread out in the ice from where she went through. No water near spread to me yet. My foot was already going numb inside my boot. Paige's body must have been in shock.

"Faryn. Help. Me." Her fingers tried to grab at the ice. From her chest down she was in the river. Her lips were already blue. "I. Can't."

I looked back the way we came. Coyote stood on the river bank watching. He wasn't making any move to come out on the ice and help.

"Hold on, Paige," I said and took a step. The ice moved. My knees bent as I tried to steady myself.

"Faryn. I didn't kill Nancy." Her mouth dropped below the surface. She came up and spat. "I. Couldn't." She tried to take a breath after each word though the frozen river pressed against her.

"Just hold on, Paige. I have to find something to get to you."

"No! I was supposed to kill her." She changed her grip and her mouth dropped below again. She came back up spitting and coughing. "Nancy. Looked. Undead." Paige let go. Her body disappeared into the dark river as it pulled her under the ice toward the bridge. The current was so strong that bodies were sometimes never found when they accidentally fell in. She was gone.

I stared at the hole where Paige had been. I looked to the bank. Coyote still stood there staring out at me. I turned and dove across the ice. My body slid toward her black Smith and Wesson. I grabbed the gun, got up on one knee, turned to the river bank and brought the weapon up.

Coyote ran through the willows.

With a growl I brought the gun back and pushed to my feet. I couldn't shoot him. He didn't have a weapon and he wasn't a threat at that moment.

I looked at the spot where Paige had gone under. It was already starting to freeze over. I was halfway across the river with a lot more to go. I couldn't dwell on her. She did bad things to people and at this moment something bad could be happening to others.

As I started toward the far side I heard a car engine. Coyote was going to be across the river in seconds. He could be at Grady's in minutes.

Chapter 70

PAIGE WAS DEAD. MY boot hit an ice peak. I put my hands on another. Water gurgled up. Move.

Gazing up at the bridge I couldn't see the car. Did he turn already? He could be at Grady's house in just minutes and then what? He could have my gun and be waiting for me on the other side.

Red lines squiggled in front of my eyes. Pain surged through my head. I raised my hands to my forehead in an attempt to help. The handgun felt cool against my skin.

Fuzzy. The fog was moving in. Stumble. Ice cracked. Run.

Step. Step. Step. My throat burned. I wretched. Step.

My boot went through the ice. It touched riverbed before water went up over the top and filled the boot. The other foot pushed up the bank. Step. My knees hit the ground. Red squiggly lines crossed my eyes. Snow. My hands hit snow. The fog was moving around my eyes. It was getting dark even with the sun out. Everything was going. Black.

Chapter 71

COLD. DARK.

Something wasn't right. I was on the ground. I blinked fast to get ice off my lashes.

Noise. I rolled to the side. My teeth came down on my lip as pain shot around my back.

A something large rumbled across the bridge.

Where was Coyote?

I scrunched my toes in my boot. They were the only part of me not cold. It wasn't anything. My one foot was numb.

I looked down past my feet to the river. The hole my foot had made was almost frozen over. How long had I been lying there?

Walk, Faryn.

I got to my knees. I picked Paige's gun off the ground before getting all the way up. There was darkness all around the edges of my vision like a fuzzy picture frame on a graphic app. I was walking into a tunnel.

I got up on the side road and headed away from the bridge. The snow that had been falling had drifted across making it a sheet of white. What was missing? Tracks. Tire tracks. There were none going through the snow in either direction. The snow could have drifted over them after Coyote drove this way.

How long was I out?

Emery was out there. Grady was her defender. They needed me.

Tree. I put my shoulder against the poplar before my face could go into it. I had walked off the road. How did that happen? I started walking again.

I had killed Paige. I didn't know if she was trying to kill me or not, so was it in self defense or was it homicide? She was a fellow officer. How was I supposed to go to headquarters and face the other officers after killing one of our own?

My knees hit the ground. The tunnel was getting smaller.

I stood. Red lines waved across my vision again. The frame was getting thicker.

The huge house was in front of me. How long was I walking? Did I go in the right direction?

There were no cars. There should have been a yellow Volkswagen Beetle and the dented truck. Paige's car wasn't there. Where were they? They raped them, killed them and left. They wanted me to find them to continue my torture. The pictures, the banging my walls, the emails...it wasn't enough. Beating Jimmy was a tease. This was the final act.

I dragged my feet up the front steps. The gun dropped. I reached for the door. It opened. The world leaned.

"Faryn?"

Sky. White. Gone.

Chapter 72

BISSON GAVE ME A BIG grin as he walked in my hospital room. "How are you feeling?"

"Like the defensive line of the Roughriders ran over me then backed up and did it again a dozen times."

"That'll have to be good enough." Bisson turned to the door and gave a nod.

Delaney walked through the door with his notebook and pen at the ready. "Fuck. There goes your pretty looks."

As I moved I discovered there was no part of my body that didn't hurt. I looked up at him. My vision was still a bit fuzzy. "I got a broken nose and jumped from a moving car. What's your excuse for being ugly?"

"Funny."

Blood on a shoe. I pushed to sit up again, this time accepting the pain. "Emery and Grady?"

Bisson pushed the button to raise the hospital bed to have me half sitting. "They're out in the waiting room."

"You can talk to your fuck buddies later," Delaney ignored the Sergeants glare, "we need to know what happened."

I looked at the door then to each of them. The shoes? "Is Coyote in custody? What about the others?"

"Who? We don't know shit."

Bisson put his hand up to quiet Delaney. "You've been unconscious since you passed out at your friend's doorstep five hours ago. You lost blood, have a concussion, frostbite on your fingers, face, foot and lower back, where you're also missing skin. And you were hypothermic. You were lucky you made it as far as you did. We followed your tracks back to the bridge, but still don't know where you came from and you had Constable Garrett's service pistol with you. Let's start with, where is Paige Garrett?"

I stared up at him and felt a rush of everything. Nothing was how it seemed anymore. "In the river. She tried to kill me. I think she tried to kill me." I rubbed tears from my cheeks. Paige's handcuffs had worn grooves into my wrists that were now a dark colour. My fingertips tingled. "Do you guys have the shoes?"

"Slow down, Faryn. What do you mean Paige is in the river?"

I took a few breaths. They hurt. "Paige back fist me, breaking my nose, then handcuffed me. I thought they were taking me to Grady's house to kill me, so I jumped from the car on the other side of the bridge. She chased me onto the ice. She had her gun pulled, so I had every reason to think she was going to kill me. We fought and she went through the ice. I was going to try to save her but she let go."

"Do you have the box of shoes?"

"Constable Garrett went through the ice? What time was this?"

"Um, I think the dashboard said 1:15 before I jumped from the car. I couldn't save her."

"You jumped from this car at quarter after one?" Delaney had been writing everything. "You didn't show up at your fuck buddies until almost three. Where were you all that time?"

"I didn't get there until when? What time is it now?" There was no light around the window curtains.

"Faryn! Where were you?"

"Did you get the damn shoes? Paige was supposed to call Ident." She didn't though. She had lied to me about that and my link to Nancy Harrelson and all the others was lost. "Someone has to get to the Stable and secure the barn."

"Who gives a shit about shoes. Where the hell were you?"

"Calm down, Constable," Bisson's voice was firm enough he didn't have to look at the officer to shut him up. "Corporal Steel, give Constable Delaney your full statement starting from when you left the Wakaw detachment. That's the last place we have you. We put out a Be-On-the-Lookout-For for Constable Garrett's car after Constable Faye came to me and said she left you in Wakaw and couldn't get in contact with you. I'm going to call about getting people in the river and I'll have to call internal affairs." Bisson lifted his phone and headed for the hallway.

Chapter 73

"KNOCK, KNOCK," GRADY actually knocked as he said it and opened the door to poke his head through. "Is Constable Porn Stache gone?"

Laughing hurt. Delaney got his statement and then left. "Yeah, come in."

He opened the door and let Emery walk in first. She put a purple teddy bear on the bedside table and awkwardly leaned down to kiss my cheek. "Oh my God, Faryn. Look at your beautiful face. Are you in a lot of pain?"

"Not a lot. They have me on some good drugs."

"You scared the crap out of me."

"Both of us," Grady squeezed my calf. "I saw something coming down the driveway. Never thought it was you. You had so much blood on you I thought it was a zombie movie."

"Were they ever there," I asked.

"Who?"

Both of them wore bewildered expressions. "Pony, River, Dove, Coyote, Paige, anyone. They were never there were they?"

"No, nobody came to the house."

"But they were taking me there." I looked at Emery. "They had your Loubies. There was blood on them."

"What are you talking about, Faryn?"

They lured me in like a sucker fish and I took the bait. Just another stab at me. "They're a cult. They attack and rape people because they think anger and jealousy are pure. They brutalized women and men. When they're done they take a pair of the victims shoes. They had a pair of Christian Louboutin shoes like yours with fresh blood on them. I," leapt in head first, "I jumped to the conclusion that it was you. I got in their car and they drove right toward your place. I thought you might have both been dead. Fuck." I put myself right in front of them with blinders on. I saw what they wanted me to."

"Faryn, did they take the pictures of us?"

I nodded. "It was all about me. In their twisted beliefs I wasn't doing something right."

"Is Emery safe?"

How do I answer that question? Between the river and being in the hospital and talking to Delaney and Bisson seven hours had passed. In that time Coyote could have been in Calgary. He could be in the United States by then. The Portal, North Dakota boarder crossing was only 5 hours from Saskatoon. They could have gotten on a plane and could be just about anywhere. "Our guys will catch them," was all I could think of to say. The old saying was that we always got our man. I wished it was that simple.

Chapter 74

THE DOOR OPENED JUST a little. A voice came through with a fake Jamaican accent. "Faryn, ya dead?"

Only one thing I could answer with, "yah man."

"I told you!" Brandi jumped through the door pointing at me. "I told you, I told you, I told you. I told you Paige was henky."

I would have rolled my eyes if it wasn't going to hurt so much. "Yeah, yeah."

"Damn. You look like that Smurf that got bit by a fly and turned purple and kept biting the other Smurfs."

The center of my face was a swollen purple mess. My vision was still fuzzy because of swollen cheeks getting in the way. I was told by a nurse that my backside was a kaleidoscope of colour as the bruising all came out. Every limb had mottled patches of dark purple and blue. "I'm taking that as a compliment."

"Has there been any word on the bad guys yet?"

"Every cop in three provinces are looking for Coyote. Delaney brought Pony in, but I don't know if anything will come of it. I haven't heard if they found Paige's body yet?"

Brandi pulled a chair close to my bed. She gave my untouched food tray a once over. "Not yet, is what I heard. She went under the ice and that river has a wicked current. A couple divers went in, but they pulled them out because it wasn't safe. What's wrong?"

I stared up at the ceiling. By now every cop knew what had happened. I was too tired and sore to be tough, so I let the tears flow. "I killed her."

"She would have killed you. I heard what happened, Faryn, and I don't think you had a choice. You were handcuffed. She broke your nose. She killed Nancy Harrelson, right?"

"No, she didn't. Her last words were that she didn't shoot her."

"Faryn, she was lying."

"She was already in the water. She had no reason to lie. I really don't think she did it. I don't think she shot her."

"Then Coyote did it."

My lips twisted. "He doesn't have the guts. Paige said something though that got me thinking. If I give you some names can you get them into headquarters tomorrow?"

"It's my day off."

"Come on, I need you. They're holding me over night for observation, so I can't be there until around noon and even then I might have to break out of here. Get them in, please." I scribbled the names on a pad I had borrowed from a nurse earlier.

She got to her feet and took the paper. "Fine. You'll just owe meme. Yet again. The Man is waiting downstairs, so I will see you later. Get some rest."

DAY SEVEN
SUNDAY

Chapter 75

MY WHOLE BODY ACHED as I lowered myself into a chair at headquarters.

Over night River and Dove got picked up trying to hide in Saskatoon. After a few hours of being interviewed they corroborated what Coyote and Paige had said about Omega.

Dove admitted that it was her idea to use the drug scopolamine on Pony. With that drug anyone could be told to do something and they would do it without question and without remembering a thing. There was a case out west in Middleton, B.C. where victims of a serial killer cut pieces off of other victims and ate them. They had Pony be with the women, and in some cases rape the women, just in case they ever needed someone to take the blame. Some of the first victims already had sex with him before their attack, so continuing it was easy.

River found it hilarious that we would never know how many members of Omega were out there. "Oh my God, you guys really think we were just all sitting around some stupid farm? You cops are pretty pathetic."

"Is that what you think?" Delaney sat across the table from her. The video of the interviews had been waiting on my computer. "This looks pretty pathetic." He showed her a photograph. A copy of that was also on my desk. It was a still Vista was able to get from my neighbour's Cheryl's security video. A copy was on my desk. "Isn't that you walking across the street from Corporal Steel's house? That's the night someone broke in."

"Sucks to be her."

Delaney smiled. "Considering we found the Corporal's gun in one of your bags, it sucks to be you."

I shut the video off the moment River started crying.

There was still no word on Coyote. Paige's car was found on the side of the road inside the Sturgeon Lake reserve, but that didn't mean anything. He could have switched vehicles long before that. We would find him.

"First let me say I'm sorry about my appearance. It's been a long twenty-four hours. What do you boys think? Do I look like a zombie?" Andy and Zeke Thompson-Bing stared across the interview table at me. Their parents sat to one side.

"Corporal Steel, are you going to tell us what this is about?"

I stared at Mr. Thompson for a moment. "I'll get to it." I returned my attention to the boys. "When I was young I spent some of my summers at my grandmother's place. We didn't have video games and cell phones then, so I was always playing outside. I would run around the sheds with her dogs and pretend we were getting chased. Sometimes I went in the woods and used my imagination like I was trying to track someone down. I guess I was always going to be a cop. Do you guys ever do that? Use your imaginations? It seems to be a lost art these days."

Zeke and Andy played with their fingertips trying to rub black smudges off. Their mother reached into her purse and handed both of them a wet wipe to help with the fingerprint ink. "Sometimes, I guess," Zeke said.

I moved and suppressed a groan. "My favorite thing to do was go exploring. Just letting my imagination go and find things, see how they worked or what they were." I paused for a moment. My body was at that place where all the muscles were tense. Pain killers only did so much. "People say kids don't have imaginations these days. That video games and TV shows are taking that away. What do you guys think?"

Both boys shrugged simultaneously. Shining.

"What I think is that games and shows and movies fuel the imagination. They show you things you never even thought of and let your mind go wild." The door behind me opened. I struggled to half turn before I saw Brandi. She nodded and handed me a paper that I glanced at it and pulled myself back to be facing the boys. "But imaginations can get away from us. Last Sunday you told your mom that you found, a zombie, a dead woman, right? I'm not that into the genre. Aren't zombies and the dead two different things?"

The boys looked at each other before Zeke answered with a timid, "I guess."

"Your mom said you had been wearing your hunters orange vests whenever you left the property. You both wore them last Sunday, didn't you? I had Constable Faye pick them up today when the officers escorted you in. You said you didn't go near the body right, but there is dried blood on your vests."

"We go hunting," Mr. Thompson said quickly, "it can get bloody."

"You told me yesterday that you haven't gone hunting this year. We are testing the blood now though. What Constable Faye handed me is the boys fingerprints." The parents were clicking in. Their faces were tight with worry and the realization of what I was saying. "There was a fingerprint found on the shotgun that was next to the body. We compared it to the boys. No match."

The father let out a sigh of relief. "What the hell is all this? I mean, why are we even here?"

I was staring at the boys mother. She was watching her children with that love in her eyes I never saw as a kid. I saw it from other moms towards my friends, I wanted it, but I never got it. A look could mean so much. "Mrs. Thompson-Bing, I'd like to have your fingerprints taken."

Tears fell from her eyes. Her sons looked at her. "They were playing a game. They didn't know what they did. I tried wiping the gun down like the crime - like they do on TV. It's not like they did it on purpose."

"Why are you crying Mommy?" Andy grabbed her hand.

"We didn't do anything wrong." Zeke pushed his chair back and stood up.

Mr. Thompson couldn't fix his gaze on anyone. "What did you do? Boys, what did you do?"

Andy started crying in sobs. "It was a zombie, Daddy. It reached for me."

"I protected him," Zeke wasn't crying. The young boy was mad. "I shot the zombie. I killed it." He looked at his dad wanting things to be okay. "I didn't do anything wrong."

Chapter 76

"SO?" I LOOKED UP AT Brandi from my desk chair as she stepped up.

"The mother's left index matches the print on the gun stock. Do you think her story is legit?"

"I do," I said. A real mother protected her children from anything. Even something they did that she knew was wrong. "She panicked and did what she thought was right. I can't fault her for that." I tossed a pen. It bounced off a bottle of pain meds and landed on my keyboard. "Paige was telling the truth. If I had just asked more questions or looked at those vests she wouldn't be dead. They wouldn't have come after me."

"Bullshit. The kid finished Nancy Harrelson off, sure, but she was still brutally assaulted. She was raped, beaten, traumatized. You would have to go after whoever did that, which would have put you in the exact place you are now. There was a bunch of wackados out there raping and taking shoes. Paige made her own bed and she chose to leave the side of the law. Delaney found pictures of Nancy Harrelson at different steps of her attack at Paige's apartment. She was all in. Faryn, they told you what they had done. There was only one way out of that. Somebody was going to die."

"She's right," Bisson walked from his office. "The box of shoes was still at the Stable. Every pair of shoes was likely a victim of this group. We will have to work through the loft pictures and see if we can match them to victims. Now we know about Omega and this Coyote has no place to hide."

I had watched all of the interviews of the known Omega members. Everything started with Coyote. He raped Marta St. John because he wanted her when they both worked at the Greek. He followed her to the Stable and then couldn't handle Pony getting what he wanted. Naomi Fuller was attacked because River was in love with Pony and jealous of the women he was with. The jogger allegedly attacked Dove. Anger, jealousy, hate, it all brought on pain and didn't resolve a thing.

"I've been talking to Internal Affairs. They still have to do their official investigation, but you did the right thing and I don't see any charges coming against you. You should go home and rest. Your officially off of work until you've healed. Go home."

"Yeah," the groan couldn't be left in as I stood up. "I don't really want to be there anymore."

Bisson smiled at me. "That's something for you to deal with."

LATER

Chapter 77

IN CONTRAST TO THE shiny creamed-coffee coloured log walls the support column of the house was the natural tan of the inside of a tree. It had been cut into three hexagons. The top and bottom ones were long and smooth with a smaller one in the middle sticking out slightly in all directions. It had been worn darker just beneath the middle hexagon from children's hands grabbing onto it as they ran around. Playing. Here and there were vertical cracks, one big enough to put a finger in. Sandra Kissler used the natural lines and knots of the former tree to draw pictures of animals on the surface. A bunny rabbit had a knot for its little nose. Over time she carved them out just a little so they stood out and Kenneth told me he used a burning tool to make the outlines black. I traced the neck of a swan with my finger.

"Excuse me, Faryn" The Man had sweat on his brow. He had my small dining table in his hands. I grabbed the column as I stepped into the sunken living room to let him pass to the dining room.

Grady came behind with a dining chair in each hand.

"I wish you guys would let me help."

The Man shrugged and headed back out to the truck. Grady kissed my cheek before saying they had it and followed the other man.

Emery walked in next. She wasn't her regular made-up self today. She was natural. She put a box on the kitchen counter. "Your new place is beautiful, Faryn. I'm so happy for you." I didn't know if the three of us would ever have our fun again, but at least they were talking to me.

"What did your nosey neighbor say about you moving?" Brandi carried in grocery bags. "Everybody want tea?"

"Sure. I kind of left Cheryl speechless." I walked to the wood fireplace and held my hands above the blue metal barrel which was the main base. The first thing Grady did when we got out there was start a fire. The same day we discovered who really shot Nancy Harrelson I contacted a realtor about buying the Kissler house. My place in the city was now on the market. "I saw Cheryl was watching when the realtor was appraising the house, so I went over to her. I apologized to her and asked if I could talk to Wendell, her son. I gave him my business card with my cell number written on the back and told him if he ever needed anything to give me a call and then I kissed him."

"No? You kissed him?" Emery took mugs from the box.

I looked out a tall thin window at the back deck and a small grassy hill in front of the woods. I nibbled on my bottom lip for a second. "Okay, I made out with him. My tongue curled his toes and his mom was left speechless and jealous."

Brandi said, "you slut." She took a fresh bottle of Captain Morgan from the bag.

Pony had been in touch. He wanted to help me with my demons. Almost everyone had left the Stable and the families of Omega victims were taking him to court. He was looking for anyone to be on his side. I wasn't that person.

Emery held a couple mugs up. "Faryn, which do you want? The Eeyore mug or Wile E. Coyote?"

END

Author's Note

I DISTINCTLY REMEMBER saying, when I was a teenager, that I never wanted to move to Saskatchewan. I grew up around thick forests and rocky hills. My favorite pastime was to walk into the woods and not get home until sunset. Saskatchewan was prairie. Flat fields of gold going on forever, highways that reached to the horizon in a straight line. I didn't know that the farther north you went the more it looked like home. Careers brought us to the province and this was where we made our new home. The setting for my first novel, Red Island, came from our then home, Prince Edward Island and for Not What it Seems Saskatchewan seemed to be the place where it had to happen. The body in this book was found in the field behind our property, the Stable is based on our actual property and a lot of the places are real places. I won't say I've grown to love Saskatchewan but I have grown to appreciate its beauty and have been inspired.

A book is only as good as the people you can get your research from and I had a few that I owe a huge debt of gratitude to. Whether it had to do with police work or coroner duties, publishing or threesomes I thank them over and over for their knowledge.

Even when a writer finishes a book they really don't Know if it is any good. I don't anyway. I had some readers check it out, find plot holes and help me fix things up. Different people with different backgrounds who each gave me a new outlook into what I created and helped me learn. And I still don't know if it is any good. I think it is. I enjoyed reading it, so I hope you did. Please let me know either way. If you liked it please drop a review and if you didn't please email me and let me know what you didn't like. Lorneoliverauthor@gmail.com

After this note you are going to find the recipes for the pulled pork sandwich Faryn brings to Vista. I'm a chef by trade, so it wouldn't be me without adding some food in here. It's something I started with The Cistern paperback and something I enjoy doing. The only rule I have about recipes is, make it work for you. This isn't baking and you're not building a Space Shuttle. Adjust the recipes to your taste. I don't know what you like.

The final thing I want to say is about the support of my family. While I was writing this novel my family grew with the birth of my grandson and a lot of my time has been with him and seeing the world through his eyes. I complain about it but what I love most is when he insists on me lifting him up when I'm cooking so he can see what I'm doing. Little bugger is not a fan of the book editing process however. My whole family is in this book, in every book in one way or another, and without them this is all nothing.

Last note. I love Easter eggs in movies and novels. They are those little things that the author knows about and hopefully fans will pick up on. Like always, there are a few connections to my other novels...see if you can find them...and to things I am a fan of. If you figure out who or what was the inspiration for Pony shoot me an email.

Be safe my friends. Be shiny.

PULLED PORK

GET YOURSELF A 5LB or so pork roast. Shoulder is good.

3 tablespoons - smoked paprika

1 tablespoon – garlic powder

2 tablespoons – brown sugar

1 tablespoon – dry mustard

3 tablespoons – salt

1 tablespoon – chipotle mango (not easy to find. Omit if you can't)

2 teaspoons – black pepper

1 teaspoon – chili powder

Mix all of the seasonings into a bowl. Put the pork into a roasting pan and rub the rub all over the pork like you want to make it feel good. Massage it into the meat and get it all over. Make sure the pork fat is on the top so as it melts the fat moistens the meat.

Put it in a 300 degree preheated oven for about 6 hours. It may differ depending on the meat and oven and who knows what else. Basically you want it to fall apart easily. Take it out of the roasting pan and let rest about 10 minutes or so, then while the meat is still hot take 2 forks and pull the meat apart. Just shred it.

You can always freeze some for use later. Toss what you are going to use in either your favorite barbecue sauce (Sweet Baby Ray's is A-mazing) or make the sauce recipe you'll find in this book. Get a good Kaiser bun or pretzel bun and put a healthy amount of meat on it. Add some of the apple slaw and eat.

BARBEQUE SAUCE

STEP 1, PUT EVERYTHING in a pot on your stovetop and turn to medium heat.

Step 2, stir it until butter is completely melted and everything is incorporated.

Step 3, cool it. Use it on whatever meat you want.

1 cup – butter

4 cups ketchup

¼ cup brown sugar, packed

½ cup apple cider vinegar

1 tablespoon – paprika

2 tablespoons – garlic powder

1 tablespoon – onion powder

4 teaspoons – Cajun seasoning

1 teaspoon cayenne

¼ cup – Worcestershire sauce

2 teaspoons – liquid smoke

1 tablespoon – chipotle mango (see not in pulled pork)

3 tablespoons – molasses

APPLE SLAW

2 CUPS – RED CABBAGE, sliced thinly
    1 cup – green cabbage, sliced thinly
    1 Granny Smith apple, cut into matchsticks
    1 cup – carrots, grated
    3 green onions, sliced long and thin
    2 tablespoons – olive oil
    2 tablespoons – honey
    2 tablespoons – apple cider vinegar
    Juice of 1 lime
    Zest from that 1 lime
    ¼ teaspoon – red pepper flakes
    Salt and pepper to taste

Prep all of the veg and apple. In a bowl mix everything else together. Toss in the prepped stuff. Boom. Done. If you let it sit in the fridge for a little while the flavors will develop more.

ABOUT LORNE OLIVER

LORNE OLIVER'S SEARCH history reads something like this: what happens to an eyeball after it's out of the body, what do high heels do for a woman, Canadian gun laws, fudge brownie recipe, how to write a good "about the author page," best way to get rid of a body in Saskatchewan in January at 3:30pm on a Tuesday, how do you delete your search history? After culinary school he and his wife traveled across Canada and back again with their two children, finally settling in Saskatchewan where their family grew to include a grandson, nine dogs, a couple cats and a bunch of chickens. He continues to work as a chef in the far north of the province and writes every chance he can.